Run or Submit

Run or Submit

David Moreau

ROBERT HALE · LONDON

ISBN 0 7090 6384 9

Robert Hale Limited
Clerkenwell House
Clerkenwell Green
London EC1R 0HT

2 4 6 8 10 9 7 5 3 1

Typeset in North Wales by
Derek Doyle & Associates, Mold, Flintshire.
Printed in Great Britain by
St Edmundsbury Press, Bury St Edmunds, Suffolk.
Bound by WBC Book Manufacturers Limited, Bridgend.

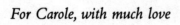

For Carole, with much love

Warm thanks to
David and Phyllis Morgan
for electronic help and
encouragement

Chapter 1

A stone humpback bridge loomed up. A medieval one that the pack-mules used to plod over on their week-long journey to Italy. Fairfax Rhys reflected that this was by far the best time of the day for his sort of helicopter flying. He had left Zurich–Kloten airfield at first light, knowing that then he could indulge safely in his favourite sport of hedge-hopping without so much chance of being reported, even in Switzerland, where early rising and telling things to the police were both national customs. Unfortunately, his metabolism needed hair's-breadth escapes as those of some men crave drink or drugs. And the fact that he had earned his living for nearly twenty years crashing aircraft, cars and his own battered but well-healed body into various solid objects in front of the cine cameras had done nothing to cure him.

'If anything it's bloody well made me worse,' he muttered to himself, swerving round a plantation of pines, misty with vaporizing dew. But he couldn't go on indefinitely like this. After being sent down from the university, he had discovered that the same wild driving habits that had finished his chances of getting a degree could in fact make a profession that was several times more lucrative than the Foreign Service for which his parents had destined him. From then on, his whole life had been cheerfully organized around the possibility of his death or maiming on any day of the week. No wife, no house, no real roots anywhere. And, over the years, his high earning capacity had been evenly matched against an equally spectacular spending ability.

He eased the stick back to leap over a road bridge that crossed the valley. So far he had seen no traffic, although it was June and the holiday rush had just begun on the vaulted motorway above him to his left. Then, as he dipped back towards the valley bottom and the old road, he noticed a yellow E-type Jaguar coupé racing along nearly on a level with him but about a hundred yards away to his left.

He decided to climb fifty feet, professionally concerned not to distract a fellow spirit who was clearly taking the narrow, winding road at about the limit of safety anyway. The car was curtsying through the bends, brake lights winking briefly before the driver put the power on and slid the back end so that it cleared the low stone walls on either side with a margin of millimetres.

Fairfax reflected that driving like that was only possible on an empty road, in a superb car and by a driver who was both an expert and slightly demented. Despite the car's speed, he was gaining easily on it because the Alouette was climbing at about 90 m.p.h., whereas the car was averaging a few miles an hour less.

Fairfax was about to inch his throttle forward and leave the Jaguar behind, when he saw another car. It was silver grey, one of the latest six-cylinder Porsches, and moving so spectacularly fast that it had already almost caught the leading car. Fairfax could see that both drivers had Zurich licence plates. Must be two friends racing. Hell, but they could both drive.

Glancing swiftly round to make sure that there were no pylons or rocky outcrops looming ahead, Fairfax moved to his left so that he was directly over the two hurtling shapes. They snaked through a bend, both at the limit of their adhesion, the tyres of the Jaguar throwing up spurts of white dust as they clawed at the line of grit left from the melted spring snow.

Then, just as they began to cross another of the narrow bridges that spanned the river, the Porsche struck. Changing down with a spurt of blue exhaust into some unimaginably powerful gear, the car launched itself like the head of a striking puff-adder and drew along-side the other one. As they reached the middle of the bridge, the flanks of the two cars collided. The Jaguar driver made a frenzied attempt to wrench it back on to the road, but its sheer momentum defeated him. In a shower of sparks and masonry, he carved through the wall, and, turning languidly over and over, the car fell nearly a hundred feet, to crash in splintered wreckage on the misty bank of the river below.

His film stunt work had accustomed Fairfax to violence, and to reacting swiftly to dangerous situations. But for a moment, even he was stunned by the totally unnecessary accident he had just seen. Only for a second, however. Long before the now battered Porsche had braked to a halt at the end of the bridge, he had lost most of his forward speed and was dipping down to the narrow valley floor, searching hurriedly for a few level feet where he could land. Seeing a spot about fifty yards from the bridge, he slowed the Alouette's hurtling descent towards the dewy grass and small boulders beneath him and, having checked from close to that it was safe, dropped the helicopter on to its undercarriage, at the same time turning the power down to tickover. The Frenchman who had lent him the valu-able little aircraft would not be happy about his landing in a place like this. But then it might be a question of saving the life of at least one injured man.

Thrusting the small first-aid kit into one of the capacious pockets of his leather jacket, he opened the door and stepped down, with the momentary feeling of unreality that comes with noise-deafness in sudden silence.

The Jaguar lay smoking on its side on the riverbank, the engine just sputtering to a standstill. He ran over the rough ground towards it, not heeding the long grass which rapidly soaked his moccasins and light trousers. He had almost reached the wreckage when he heard a rock bounce down the slope as the big figure of the Porsche driver clambered over the parapet and jumped clumsily on to an outcrop below, starting the difficult descent to the river beneath.

The uppermost window of the Jaguar was broken, and the driver lay crumpled up in the coupé's luggage compartment. With one powerful wrench, Fairfax opened the battered door. The smell of petrol was overpowering. It only needed a few drops on the hot exhaust or brakes, and the car's remains would go up like a firework.

There was no time to worry about worsening the driver's injuries by moving him. Fairfax caught the band of the other's trousers and neck of his sports shirt and heaved, easing him out as gently as he could through the crumpled door arch. He had just lifted the limp form clear of the car when he heard an enraged shout in German from the Porsche driver: '*Lass' ihn, lass' ihn und geh' weg.*' Fairfax ignored it and, laying the other man gently on to the grass, felt his pulse. It was quite still. He touched the white of one of the man's eyes with his index fingernail. There was no tremor of response. He was clearly dead. More stones clattered above and behind Fairfax, followed by another furious shout and a bang which echoed languidly up and down the valley. A bullet whined angrily off the granite ten feet above Fairfax's head. Up till that moment he had still thought it conceivable that he had seen an ugly but unintentional accident. Abruptly, it was clear to him that he had witnessed a brutal murder.

He was lowering the body to the ground when something fell out of the breast pocket of the dead man's shirt. Quickly Fairfax picked it up and saw that it was a British passport in a leather folder. Another shot spat out viciously behind him, and this time the slug spattered him with chips of stone. Thrusting the passport into his jacket pocket.

Fairfax turned and ran, slithering a little on the wet grass. But in his distraction while trying to help the Jaguar driver, he had failed to notice one thing: that the gorilla-built, ginger-headed man from the other car, having come down the opposite riverbank with surprising speed, was now beginning to wade across on a course that would bring him between Fairfax and the Alouette. As the other splashed forward, he shouted in German, 'Give me back whatever it is that you have just stolen from him.'

Fairfax, realizing that the slope on his right was too steep to allow a safe detour up it on the way to the aircraft, slowed his run, then dropped hurriedly behind a small rocky outcrop as the other man stopped his stumble over the slippery stones in the river-bed and raised his gun arm. One of his two shots ripped a strip of leather out of the arm of Fairfax's jacket. He flattened himself further against the ground, feeling round for a stone to hurl. As he did so, something bulky in his inside pocket dug into his chest, and in a flash he remembered that he had thrust a miniature Very pistol and half-a-dozen cartridges in there, offered him by the Alouette's owner in case he got into trouble in the mountains.

Pulling out the little pistol, he rammed a red rocket down the muzzle and pointed it at the man in the water. He knew that the trajectory would be anything but flat, so aimed over the man's head, hoping that the flare would at least pass close enough to deter him from coming on.

The gun banged and its rocket fizzed away over the intervening thirty yards, gaining speed as it travelled. Fairfax had never aimed a Very pistol at anything very precise before, and he now watched with astonishment as the rocket only failed to make a bull's-eye because the ginger-headed man, bellowing with rage, fell to one knee in the glacial water. Fizzing and crackling fiercely, the rocket stuck in the grassy bank on the far side. Smiling with the grim satisfaction of one who enjoyed defending himself Fairfax rolled sideways and reloaded with a green rocket. The ginger-headed man had fired his last two shots and was clawing another magazine out of the breast pocket of his black suit.

Seeing his chance, Fairfax stood up, took careful aim, and sent another rocket whistling off. This one caught the other man full in the chest and sat him down, winded and probably burnt, in the shallow water. Fairfax did not wait to see how badly hurt the other might be. Turning, he raced for the Alouette, regretting bitterly as he scrambled into the cockpit that it took at least thirty seconds to get it off the ground even when, as now, the rotors were still turning. In the few spare seconds, he glanced round, wondering why the perspex was not starring with a hail of small calibre bullets. Then he saw that the man in the water was shouting up to some more figures standing along the parapet of the bridge, they and their vehicle dim shadows behind the pall of black smoke that was now dirtying the sweet morning air above the Jaguar's wreckage. As Fairfax looked, there was a flash and a bang from up on the bridge. A heavy-calibre bullet clanged against one of the struts of the undercarriage. More shots cracked out as Fairfax yanked at the throttle and screamed skywards like an express lift.

Chapter 2

Campione d'Italia lies across the dark lake from Lugano, right at the foot of the sugar loaf-shaped Monte Generoso. It is an island of Swiss territory surrounded on three sides by Italy, the fourth side being the lake. To get into it by land, you pass one symbolic but bored Italian Customs official, but there is too much local gratitude for the prosperity that the Campione Casino brings for him ever to molest the visitors who drive over the long stone bridge further down the lake and travel through Italy on the lakeside road.

Fairfax didn't arrive in quite the style of the others. He puttered along under the hot afternoon sun on a miniature motor cycle, so tiny that it spent its life stowed in the luggage compartment behind the helicopter's seat. The aircraft's owner, an eccentric and rich stunt-man, had found this solution to the feeling of helplessness that a private airman gets as soon as he lands. Its inflatable seat was surprisingly comfortable, however, and it went rather rapidly. The Italian Customs on duty glanced idly at the French registration plate and waved him on. He followed the road as it rose and fell over the lake headlands, past the big white villas with balustraded terraces built out over the water, coasting down finally into Campione and stopping in front of the Hotel Eden, standing alongside the casino on the quay. The car-park attendant gave him a queer look as he parked the diminutive bicycle confidently among the Cadillacs, Rolls and Maseratis that already stood there, then, carrying the little leather bag that was his only luggage, he walked rapidly through the swing doors and into the foyer.

'*Ah Monsieur Fairfax, enchanté de vous revoir,*' said the white-tied man at the reception, '*vous vous portez bien?*'

'*Oui merci, et vous-même?*' answered Fairfax automatically, taking his key with a smile. Abstracted, he turned quickly and stepped out to walk to the lift, colliding heavily with a tall girl who was standing just behind him.

'Oh, I'm so sorry, *mademoiselle,*' he said, catching her as she collapsed towards the terrazzo flooring.

'Why it's Fairfax, behaving like an accident-prone oaf as usual,' she said, gathering herself up.

He took a good look at her for the first time, then said, 'It's Sally Everitt, isn't it? Very clumsy of me. I'm afraid that I was thinking of something else. What are you doing down here anyway?'

'I've come here for a combined holiday and nervous breakdown after working on a film. And you?'

'Just about the same. Look, Sally, why don't you come and have a drink with me? I'm going to ask you to help with a problem I've got.'

'All right. I don't happen to be doing anything at the moment. What's the problem – wenches as usual?'

Although the remark was said mockingly, he now remembered quite clearly the last time that they had met. It was on location in Athens, the day before he had flown home, his contribution ended. He had taken her out for the evening to a night-club. They had seemed to get on very well, and he had taken her back to the unit's hotel full of expectations. But she had allowed him one swift, hard kiss outside her bedroom, then had backed through the door. Unused to refusal in his facile world, he had gone groping into the dark room after her. Then a most unprecedented thing had happened: a small but determined handful of knuckles had hit him a blow in the solar plexus like a kick from a mare as she snapped out, 'No is no, Fairfax, where are your manners?' You couldn't help but admire her. It had certainly made a more vivid recollection than just adding further to the one-night lie-ins of his life.

Now they walked down the black marble corridor to the bar that looked out over the lake. He glanced at her. She was a tall, patrician-looking girl, with smooth, dark hair that clung round her brown, unmade up face. Her height was accentuated by her tight cerise blouse and white trousers of a dermal closeness.

He was anxious not to explain what had happened until they were settled out of earshot of the other guests, in the anonymity of the bar, so he took up her previous remark and said, 'Wenches? Why should I have trouble with them? Never touch them.'

'It might not be so much what *you*, do, it's what *they* do. With only a few exceptions they find it difficult to resist scarred, devil-may-care car-wreckers like you. However, I'm glad to hear that for once they're not your problem.'

The waiter arrived, looking down his scimitar nose as he took Fairfax's order for a San Pellegrino and brightening a little with Sally's for a jumbo Campari. Fairfax waited until the man had moved out of earshot, then said, 'I saw a man murdered this morning.'

'Oh yes,' said Sally without looking up, 'which one of the gang was doing the continuity?'

'No, ducky, not in a film. A nasty and destructive real-life murder.'

Sally glanced up quickly.

'Where? Here in Campione? Are you serious?'

'Not only am I serious, but I'm suspected of having done it.'

He outlined briefly what he had seen from the Alouette that morning, adding, 'I behaved like a clot, I suppose, taking off like that. And, furthermore, after I'd picked up this doctor chap's passport I stuffed it into my pocket, and now I've prevented the Swiss

17

from identifying the body, and they want me for the murder as well.'

'You're wanted? Don't be so silly. How could you be?'

'All right. How good's your German?'

'Adequate. Why?'

Wordlessly Fairfax pulled out a copy of the *Züricher Abendblatt*.

Across the front page in the most frenzied headlines of which this rather *sotto voce* journal is capable stood the words:

HELICOPTERMORD AUF DEM GOTTHARD PASS

Sally took the paper and translated the article slowly aloud:

'A doctor, driving up the Gotthard in his Porsche, described today how he saw a man killed by the pilot of an Alouette helicopter. The aircraft swooped down on a passing sports car, hitting it with the undercarriage and forcing it off the road at a point where the pass crosses the river at a height of thirty metres. The car fell to the riverbank, killing the driver and being burned out. It is alleged to have been stolen recently from a Zurich street, and the man driving it has not been identified. He was about one metre eighty tall, dark-haired, age in late thirties. Anyone who recognizes this description and feels that they may be able to identify the dead man is requested to contact the police at Andermatt. The body was put aboard a passing ambulance, but this vehicle has now added to the mystery by disappearing completely.

EXCHANGE OF SHOTS

The doctor witness, Doctor Ruppert Ulicke, whose Porsche was itself damaged while avoiding the other car, told the police that the helicopter landed immediately afterwards by the wreckage, and the pilot removed some papers from the body before taking off again. Dr Ulicke, with no thought for his own safety, descended to the wreckage to try to give assistance, but was fired on and wounded by the helicopter pilot, who appeared to be using some kind of rocket weapon. The doctor fired back in self-defence, but was unable to prevent the helicopter taking off. As it left, travelling south at high speed, the *gendarmerie* arrived from Andermatt. Because of smoke from the burning car, they were unable to read its full identification number before it took off, but it appeared to be registered in France.

A GANG KILLING

It is believed that this affair may be a settling of international accounts between gangsters. The Kriminalpolizei are treating the investigation as a murder, and are very anxious to interview the pilot of the helicopter. He is described as being one metre eighty-five in height, powerfully built, dark-haired and dressed in white sports trousers and a black leather jacket.

If identified, he is likely to be dangerous, and the public is recommended not to approach him, but to call the nearest police station. All airports have been requested to contact the police immediately if an Alouette attempts to land, and similar requests have been made to other European countries through Interpol.'

'Sometimes I doubt whether you are safe to be let out on your own, Fairfax. Why don't you just go and tell the truth to the Swiss police?'

'Because I'm damn sure that they wouldn't believe me against the word of this bloody self-styled Good Samaritan Dr Ulicke, whoever he is. And he can show them where I hit him with a Very rocket. And he can point to the fact that I took this other chap's passport. And how the hell was I to know that it was the police who were shooting at me from the bridge? Policemen in civilized countries don't go around firing at respectable citizens. No, I tell you, I wouldn't have a leg to stand on.'

'Well, what are you going to do?'

'Find this bloody Ulicke creature, knock the blubber out of him and get him to sign a confession.'

'Really, my love, you're being melodramatic. You've been acting in too many gangster films recently.'

'No, I'm quite serious. I shall enjoy my revenge when the time comes. And this is where you come in. How do you trace a Swiss doctor?'

'You look him up in their equivalent of a medical directory. Most doctors – and probably chemists – would have one.'

'OK, let's go down to the chemists.'

'There isn't one here. The nearest is across the lake in Lugano. And the only doctor is on holiday at the moment. The one for the hotel comes across in a boat on request. There's a notice by the reception. No, I'll guarantee to get his address from directory enquiries. But if I'm going to act as an adviser on this insane project, I shall insist on doing it with the same attention to detail that drives my directors out of their tiny cinematographic minds. So, question one: may I see the passport of the man whom you saw killed?'

'Certainly.' Fairfax thrust his hand into his inside pocket, then hurriedly patted his side ones. Then the puzzled look abruptly cleared from his face as he said with relief, 'God, I remember now: I put it for safety in the map satchel of the Alouette.'

'That brings me to my next question: where is your Alouette at the moment?'

'Hidden behind a barn in the outskirts of Arogno village, up on the Monte Generoso. I often stay in this hotel, so I knew the hinterland up there well enough. I usually land here on the Campione airstrip. But when I heard Kloten airfield shouting over the R/T for me to report my position, I realized that I was in trouble and came down in a farm orchard at about three thousand feet. An old farmer helped me to tow the thing into the yard at the back of his barn, I gave him a hundred francs rent in advance and came on down here on the helicopter's collapsible motorcycle. How's that?' He looked proud of himself.

'Terrible. How many people saw you land?'

'God knows, I took care to fly in over the precipice side of the plateau. I'd say a few children.'

'Right then, we can assume that your arrival is already the talk of the village, and some officious busybody – you know yourself how the Swiss are – has probably telephoned down to Chiasso and told the world about you. Question three: I see that you're still wearing the clothes that the police described. Haven't you got any others?'

'No.'

'Then the next thing is to get you a change. You and I are nearly the same dimensions, distributed rather differently. I can give you a pair of black jeans – why, only the other day I read in a drivelling women's magazine that it's trendy for couples to exchange their trousers. And I can lend you a man's pillar-box red sweater so that you can get out of that moth-eaten black leather. Question four: did you check into this hotel under your own name?'

'Of course. I'm well known here.'

'There's no of course about it. Old rams like you get up to all kinds of tricks when they're on their own. Well, the first thing that you've got to do is to check out again. If Kloten has a record of your taking off, I presume that you filed a flight plan saying you were going to land at Campione?'

'Yes but—'

'Look Fairfax, I want to help you, but if you honestly prefer not to throw yourself on Swiss justice, you'll have to get out of here now. I can't imagine why the place isn't already crawling with Swiss cops. Where's your luggage?'

21

He gave a battered grin and held up his small leather bag. 'Here,' he said, standing up.

The waiter hurried across, Fairfax paid, and he and Sally moved off towards the reception hall.

As they went out, Sally said, 'I've decided to allow you to ruin my holiday. Life was a bit slow, anyway – I'm too tall to interest non-Anglo Saxon males. I'd like you to go as unobtrusively as possible into the lift and go down to the garage underneath and get into the red Alfa Sprint convertible down there. It's got French tourist plates beginning TT75 something. I'll pay your bill, pack my stuff and bring you down something to change into. Keep out of sight meanwhile, won't you?'

Fairfax nodded and did as she said. But before settling into the bucket seat of the little Alfa, he went cautiously out of the garage and wheeled in Mathieu's miniature motorcycle. Even if he lost the Alouette, he could at least save something. As he moved into the oily dimness of the garage, he heard from along the lakeshore road the grimly unmistakable snoring of a police car's horn. Moving with unhurried speed so as to avoid arousing the suspicions of the elderly, spherical garage attendant, he crossed to the red Alfa, opened the boot, folded the motor cycle and pushed it carefully into the cramped space inside. Then he got into the passenger's seat, putting on an owlishly large pair of sunglasses which were propped on top of the dashboard.

When he had worked with Sally the previous year, he had admired her combination of mocking bossiness, femininity and unforced intelligence. But he led too busy a life for his interest in her to survive the break-up of that particular location group.

Five minutes passed, ticked away by the busy little clock among the dials in front of him. He felt no great anxiety. The threat to his freedom was too recent to have roused any deep instincts. But he was nevertheless relieved when Sally appeared at the bottom of the lift, a suitcase in one hand and a cluster of clothes hung over the other. She came across, glancing round warily as she did so. The attendant moved up and fussed about for a tip, taking her case and fitting it with difficulty into the boot alongside the cycle. She got in, throwing a tangle of clothes on to the luggage space behind the front seats.

'*Avez vous une carte routière du Nord de l'Italie?*' she asked the attendant.

'*Mais oui, madame,*' he answered, turning to walk back to his cabin twenty yards away.

'Get into the back now and lie down while I heap these clothes on you,' she said quickly. Fairfax obediently scrambled his big frame over the seat back and coiled himself round on one side. Scented but suffocating layers of clothing darkened out his light. He felt the girl jerk the car into gear, start the engine and swerve quickly out into the dimly perceived evening sunshine on the quay.

A police minibus stood at the bottom of the hotel steps, a blue revolving light flashing on its roof. The only person in it was the driver, who watched without curiosity as the Alfa drove by. They rounded the end of the casino and crossed the centre of the village. A police Volkswagen stood outside the other hotel. It was empty.

'Looks like we've made it this far,' Fairfax heard Sally say over her shoulder. She slowed a little so that the ripping noise of her exhaust did not draw excessive attention, then added, 'By the way, I phoned the main chemists in Lugano while I packed with the other hand. There's no Dr Ulicke in the latest edition of the Swiss medical list. So he may be more difficult to find than you think. He's not in the Zurich telephone book either, and it would be a bit of a job to look through all the other books.'

Fairfax struggled round so that he could get enough air to say, 'Well, in default of having an address to go to, I know one thing for certain: I'm going back to the helicopter. With so many cops about, the only safe way of getting out of here will be above the clouds.'

'Taking off will be fine, I'm sure,' answered the girl, 'it's the landing that bothers me.'

They passed the end of the long concrete bridge that leads half a mile over the lake from the Lugano side. To their right a huge, blood-red sun was dropping away behind the blue mountain peaks beyond Lago Maggiore, the dazzling reflection from the water flashing through the windscreen. Sally reached up for her visor, failing as a consequence to see the uniformed man who stood with his hand upraised in the middle of the road until it was too late to do anything but brake violently.

Fairfax felt himself jerked forward, crashing into the back of her seat and half-folding it up before he could stop himself. He cursed quietly as he wriggled back into his former position as unobtrusively as possible. He heard a voice say in French with a German accent, 'Where are you coming from please, *mademoiselle?*'

Without a moment's hesitation, Sally answered, 'I've come over the Gotthard from Zurich, then through Lugano. Why?'

Fairfax lay very still, breathing shallowly. 'We are looking for a dangerous fugitive,' said the man. His voice was closer now, as if he was leaning into the car. There was a pause, then he said deliberately, 'You have the sticker of the garage at the Hotel Eden in Campione. Also the back springs of your car are rather compressed. Have you a big weight in the boot?'

'Luggage for a long holiday, that's all. May I go now, please?' There came the sound of a door latch opening. Fairfax stiffened uncertainly Then the clothes above him were abruptly whipped aside. Seeing that there was little point in trying to hide further, Fairfax sat up, dishevelled and blinking. A tall, red-faced man in a grey-green uniform was leaning in through the open door, a huge, regulation-issue automatic pistol in his right hand. Fairfax noted the shiny patches in the blueing of the muzzle where the weapon was frequently cleaned and dismantled by its loving owner.

'Ah, Monsieur Fairfax, how you resemble your description. But it is perhaps not clever of you to stay in the same clothes if you wish to evade Swiss justice.' Saying this, the man moved further into the car, his olive eyes fixed steadfastly on Fairfax's face, pistol finger stiffly ready. Then he added, 'Now we will go to your helicopter; where is it hidden please?'

'I don't know what the bloody hell you're talking about,' said Fairfax. The shining barrel of the pistol now pointed at his larynx as the other man, dark-chinned face perfectly expressionless, said, 'No? Very well then. I will count up to five. And if at the end of that time you do not agree to direct this young woman to your helicopter, then I shall shoot you for resisting arrest.'

'I love the way you Swiss encourage your tourist traffic,' said Fairfax.

In a leisurely way, the man began to count, '*Un – deux – trois. . . .*'

The safety catch was manifestly already off, and Fairfax watched disbelievingly as the stubby, black-nailed index finger of the other's hand tightened visibly on the thin trigger. 'All right you murderous bastard,' said Fairfax, 'we'll show you.'

'Thank you,' said the other, climbing unemotionally into the little car and settling down in the front seat without wavering his aim for a moment from Fairfax's face.

'OK, Sally,' said the latter, 'drive on down the road to Chiasso.'

They drove for two miles in silence, then, shortly after a sharp bend, a roughly surfaced road led off to the left. 'Right, we go up here, Sally. It climbs pretty steeply, and I'm afraid that there's only a dirt surface.' Fairfax paused, then added, emphasizing the words and speaking in English, 'This reminds me of when we worked together on that film *The Pass to Nowhere*. Remember?'

Sally caught his glance in the mirror, saying non-committally, 'Yes, I remember.'

'From now on you do not speak unless I address you,' said the other man, 'and then you will only speak French. You both speak it adequately.'

Sally made no reply, but sent the powerful little car humming up the winding road. Stones clattered against the bodywork underneath, and occasionally as they swung out of corners the wheels spun with a ripping sound as they clawed for a grip. Fairfax was watching the other out of the corner of his eye for a moment of distraction which might allow a swift attack despite the cramped space under the padded fastback roof.

The valley floor receded beneath them, the road running along vertiginous ledges with no protection from the towering drop except the occasional clump of gorse on the verge. The sun had now dropped out of sight, and a blaze of colour, barred by strips of dark grey clouds, hung over the mountains to the west.

Experimentally, Fairfax made a jerky upward movement with his right hand, hastily changing it to grasping the knob of the quarter-light window beside him when the policeman's trigger finger twitched purposefully. For the second time in a few minutes, Fairfax, knowing the sensitivity of the big Browning, seriously thought that he was going to be shot.

They came up to a hairpin bend to the left. Sally was driving so fast that the other man shouted, '*Doucement, doucement, cette route est dangereuse.*' The car slithered a little on the loose grit; then, quite suddenly as it emerged from the turn, its front wheels veered drunkenly towards the verge on the inside.

'*Dieu, j'ai perdu contrôle,*' Sally shrieked. The man beside her, obviously expecting a trick, remained gazing steadfastly at Fairfax until he felt the tyres jerk over the grass bank and heard the radiator bulldozing its way through the bushes. Then, steadying the black muzzle of his gun on the seat back so that it was only centimetres from Fairfax's breastbone, he shouted, '*Idiote,*' and snatched at the wheel with his free hand.

Fairfax had kept his own eyes inside the car with a coolness which he was far from feeling. And the instant that he saw the man's eyes jerk away from him, he scythed his right arm round in a savage hand-edge blow to the thick neck, at the same time twisting his body sideways in case he misjudged and the pistol went off. As Fairfax's hand crunched against the man's vertebrae, there was a loud bang and a scraping sound from under the car, and it juddered to a halt.

Chapter 3

In the abrupt silence, Sally sat motionless for a long moment, pale as a corpse in the dashboard glow. Then she said, 'I didn't think that you could possibly do it. Well done. Poor little car. I'm afraid that I've ruined it.'

Before answering, Fairfax carefully thumbed on the safety catch of the automatic and thrust it into the pocket of his leather jacket. Then he said, 'I couldn't have done better myself. I was damn sure that we were going over the edge.'

'Do you think that you've killed him?'

The man's head had slumped forward on to the padded dashboard. The girl pulled it back by the iron-grey hair and put her ear to his chest.

'His heart's still beating quite strongly, anyway,' she said, 'I'll get out so that you can squeeze past my seat back.'

She stepped gingerly out into the tangle of crushed bushes under the car. Fairfax followed, noticing that as his weight shifted, the car rocked as if it was pivoted on some obstacle underneath. He walked round to the other door, kicked the undergrowth out of the way, then dragged the limp body out on to the trampled space.

'Tell me if you see him stirring at all while we work on the car. I'll give him another wallop if he does. I don't like him.' He bent to look under the car, saying, 'Have you got a torch somewhere? Now that the sun has gone completely, I can't see a thing underneath.'

Sally reached into the glove pocket and handed him a small lantern. Peering down its white beam, he saw that a projecting boulder, after scarring two cross members on the chassis, had jammed under the rear suspension.

'I think I can probably bounce the thing off that rock,' said Fairfax, 'but before I do, I'm afraid that you'll have to take the small risk of sitting in the driving seat and possibly careering into the valley if she goes with a run.'

'OK, I'll leave the door open ready to bale out if necessary,' said the girl, climbing back into the car and turning the front wheels against the slight resistance of the damp roots and grass so that they pointed as far as possible away from the drop ahead. In the darkness, which smelt of hot oil, brakes, crushed foliage and bruised wild mint, Fairfax moved round to the back of the Alfa.

'Right, handbrake off and into bottom gear,' he called. The engine started and ran with a burbling noise that was much louder than before. 'The exhaust pipe's copped it, that's for sure,' said Fairfax to himself. He caught hold of the bumper bar where it felt strongest, braced his legs apart, and heaved. The wheels spun in the air, tyre treads whining uselessly against the loose bramble stalks. It was impossible to bounce the car on its springs because it was so firmly grounded. Fairfax bent his knees, then slowly straightened them against the weight of the car's whole back end. It was very satisfying to feel the car slip forward an inch, then another. The bumper bar was cutting into the palms of his hands. He knew that he could only stand the pain for a few more seconds. Again the car shifted.

'Careful Sally, she's going,' he shouted hoarsely. She slowed the engine to its tickover and turned on the headlights. Then the car bounded forward, Fairfax hanging on desperately to slow it down. The front wheels at first slithered sideways, but at last the tread gripped, and the car zig-zagged towards the road above, engine screaming as the wheels spun on the dew. The ground underfoot levelled out. Sally slowed and drove carefully down the verge, stopping still facing up the hill with the engine running and the lights on.

Breathless from his efforts, Fairfax toiled up the hill to the car, calling out, 'Can you come down and help me with the body now?'

Sally didn't answer immediately and, as he got nearer, he saw that she was sitting sideways in the driving seat with her dark head buried in her hands.

'Are you all right, my love?' he asked solicitously, putting a powerful arm round her slim shoulders.

'Yes,' she said softly, 'I'll be all right in a moment. Now I know what you go through, crashing your cars.' She put an arm round his loins as he stood beside her in the darkness. A minute drifted by, then she said, 'All right, let's go,' and got slowly to her feet. He kept an arm round her shoulders as they picked their way back to where the car had stuck, the scars of the spinning wheels showing clearly where it had been. But there was no sign of the unconscious man except a brown leather wallet lying on the crushed grass.

'Hell, the swine's run off,' said Fairfax. 'I'll have a hunt for him in a minute. But first let's have a look at this.'

Picking up the wallet, he pulled out a sheaf of papers and began to leaf through them by the light of the torch. There were Swiss stamps, a photograph of two children, a few receipts, some Swiss notes and a driving licence. Inside there was a picture of the heavy-faced man who had held them up. Alongside, was the name *Herr Dr Chem. Peter Kisten, Allerheiligen Sanatorium, Gletsch, Ticino.*

'Another goddam doctor,' said Fairfax wonderingly, 'but a chemical one this time. Why am I suddenly being pursued by murderous eggheads, tell me that?'

He thrust the wallet into his pocket and added, 'I guess that a man like our doctor friend, suffering from a nasty headache and anxious to get back to civilization, would head down the valley road, rather than toiling up to a miserable mountain village, don't you? It'd be quicker to take the car, but he'd hear us coming, so I'd better have a go at catching him on foot, perhaps going cross-country. After all, I have a light and he hasn't.'

'You won't kill him or anything stupid, will you?' asked Sally.

'Of course not, darling. I just want to make sure that he can't give the alarm before daylight comes and we can take off. The place will be swarming with scientific thugs if we once let him get to a telephone.'

Pulling out the pistol, cocking it and flicking on the safety catch, he set off at a quick walk over the rough ground. The uniform that the doctor was wearing had not looked quite right for a Swiss policeman, and now he realized why. It must have been some kind of reservist soldier's uniform, which he had put on in order to look official. Could he have come over from Gletsch? It must be a couple of hours' drive over the Gotthard. It was in itself significant that the stranger had an address in the same general area as the one in which Fairfax had seen the two cars collide that morning.

Moving by the dull glow in the sky that was all that remained of the sunset, he padded through the young bracken and low undergrowth, not heeding the thorns and gorse, until he got to the high bank that dropped fifteen feet on to the road beneath. He stopped and listened. A nightingale was singing about 200 yards away. Cars and lorries hummed past on the valley road far below. A Vespa buzzed somewhere rather closer. Otherwise, there was silence; that strange, hissing mountain silence that can make a man feel uneasy. He assumed that the other man had started along the upper leg of road that ran round a hairpin bend about a quarter of a mile away to his left. That made half a mile in all. Unless he had covered the distance like an Olympic runner, he could not have passed his vantage point yet.

As Fairfax leaned forward to check how easy it would be to slither down the shale face beneath him, he heard the clink of a boot nail on a stone. The doctor had certainly been wearing heavy regulation boots. That would handicap him in the dark against Fairfax's supple moccasins. Another clink sounded much nearer, with a small spark this time. The hair at the back of Fairfax's neck prickled with anticipation.

Pushing the safety catch forward, he aimed both the gun and the torch at the source of the sound, a finger ready on the switch to bring on the beam. The man was still about thirty yards away when the toiling Vespa whirred round the nearest hairpin on the way up from the valley. Fairfax dropped to his knees. The wavering headlight caught a dark figure walking briskly down the grass verge on the extreme edge of the road, hence the relative silence of his movements. Raising his gun, Fairfax was about to line up the sights when he realized that the figure was much smaller than the uniformed man, and was wearing civilian clothes. It must, in fact, be some harmless peasant on his way home.

Congratulating himself on not having jumped the man or shot him on the spot, Fairfax backed further into the shadows. As he did so, he heard a tremendous scream from somewhere above, followed by another. Sally's voice. In a second, he was running back up the hill at top speed.

He could hear scuffling and running feet. Turning on the torch as he ran, he was just in time to see the uniformed man knock Sally over violently, then run to the Alfa and climb in, slamming the door behind him.

'Stop or I'll shoot,' shouted Fairfax, forgetting in the heat of the moment that the other spoke French. He raised the gun and fired in the direction of the car, whose distant loom he could see against the lighter sky. The shot echoed wildly round the rocks and precipices for miles around. After a momentary pause while the man found the ignition key, the starter whirred and the car leapt forward, scattering stones, and roared for the first bend. Fairfax stopped and took careful aim between the two rear lights. At the same moment, the car jerked sideways as it slid into the first bend, and his shot went wide. Panting for breath in the thin air, Fairfax ran to bend over Sally. As he reached her, to his surprise she sat up slowly.

'Are you all right?' he queried anxiously.

'Yes, I think so,' she said, 'grazed a bit, that's all. I wasn't expecting the sod to creep up on me from behind like that. Sorry I let the car go.'

'Well, at least he's gone on upwards,' he said, 'as this is the only road to Monte Generoso, he can't get down without our seeing him. And I can have another serious pot-shot at him.'

'Darling, I've just remembered, he can't get far anyway. There were only a couple of litres of petrol left when I turned up here. I was about to switch on the reserve tank. He can't get far unless he knows Alfas well enough to find the reserve tap, which is rather well-hidden.'

'Brilliant. Now, do you feel fit enough to start walking? I wasn't expecting things to get rough so soon.'

'Yes, I think so. It may surprise you to know that I am almost enjoying myself. It's a nice change from lounging in the sun on the lake shore.'

'Good girl.'

They had only walked a few steps, when the Vespa laboured round the corner behind them.

'That thing sounds horribly overloaded anyway, but I'll try to get at least one of us a lift,' he said, stepping into the road and waving his arms. The machine stopped, overheated motor puttering irregularly and headlight dimming as the dynamo slowed.

'*Cosa che?*' shouted the young man who was driving. Heaped round him were parcels and baggage, and a large suitcase was gripped between his knees.

'Someone has stolen our car and we'd like to follow him,' shouted Fairfax in French, 'could you possibly take one of us with you?'

'I'll take both of you,' said the young man, smiling with indomitable Italian helpfulness, 'the lady can sit on here' – he indicated the suitcase – 'and perhaps you can climb up here,' – he pointed to the rope-secured mound behind him – 'but we go slowly, *hein?*'

'Thanks very much,' said Fairfax doubtfully, helping Sally up, then adding his weight on the sagging suspension by the simple expedient of jumping in the air and falling face-first across the luggage, like a rescued damsel across a knight's saddle pommel.

Clutch slipping madly, the gallant scooter struggled forward, its driver shouting proudly, 'See, she is strong, no?' The speed rose slowly until they reached a wobbly ten miles per hour, beyond which the motor could not go.

'Are you all right Sally?' Fairfax shouted above the noise.

'Yes thanks,' she called back, refraining from adding that her greatest discomfort was the boy's friendly arm round her waist in a suffocating grip.

The Vespa bumped on. Fairfax was beginning to wonder how long he could bear the assorted lumps in the luggage which were digging into his abdomen. There was no possibility of shifting his position without upsetting the whole party's equilibrium. They veered round a bend. Then another. Then a third. He could smell the little two stroke getting hotter. Raising his head, he peered upwards. About 500 yards higher up the mountain, he could see a few lights. That would be the group of rough stone houses at the crossroads. You turned right to the dead-end village of Monte Generoso, and left to a mountain inn and a rough road over the mountains and to the Italian frontier.

Rolling on his side, Fairfax tapped the young driver on the shoulder and shouted, '*Au carrefour, est-ce que vous tournez à droite ou à gauche?*'

'Neither,' the other shouted back, 'I live here.' Fairfax grunted. The scooter toiled round another bend. Its wavering headlamp glinted on the rear reflector of a car, stationary at the side of the road with its boot open. In a few seconds, they were near enough for Sally to turn and shout, 'That's my Alfa ahead.'

'*Arrêtez a côté de cette voiture, s'il vous plaît*,' said Fairfax to the driver, 'the man who stole it may be still around, so watch out.' His ribs were beginning to ache from the knobbly luggage. He waited tensely for the scooter to slow down, then sprang off before anyone looking into the glaring scooter headlight could have seen anything. He ran a few steps, then wrenched open the Alfa's door. The inside was silent and empty. Sally joined him, while the scooter driver, engine chattering irregularly, stood over his machine watching them intently.

'Well, assuming that he hasn't booby-trapped it, let's drive on,' said Fairfax, 'how do you switch to the reserve tank?'

The girl climbed into the driving seat and reached under the facie to snap a switch. Then she said quietly, 'There's just one important thing missing: the ignition key. And I haven't got a spare.'

'Hell. Was the boot key attached to it, by any chance?'

'Yes.'

'Blast. I bet he went to look in the boot for a spare can of petrol, and found my little bike.' He walked quickly to the back of the car. A cluster of keys hung in the lock. The boot space was empty except for their small bags. Only a gleaming spot of oil showed where the tank of the little machine had leaked.

'Here are your keys, then,' he said, reaching in beside Sally to put them into the ignition. 'But the bike has gone. Now, if the car will start, I'll send off the scooter. Its noise will be drawing too much attention.'

'*Niente, niente, non, non*,' said the young man, fending off the twenty-franc note that Fairfax held out, '*nous sommes tous les autobilistes, hein?*'

With a wave, the young man wobbled off as the Alfa's engine turned over – and the empty carburettor filled. Then, with a thunderous bang through the hole in the exhaust, it fired. Fairfax stood warily at the side of the car, the big revolver in his hand. It had occurred to him that the man might be waiting in the darkness to see where they went. Then he climbed in. In the dashlights he could see that Sally's colour had come back, and she even looked as if she might be enjoying herself.

'You're a tough cookie, aren't you?' he said. 'I'd never have thought of casting you in the part of a fugitive's moll, but you're perfect in the part.'

She smiled quickly at him, saying, 'Try telling that to my little, old, grey-haired mum in East Grinstead. She always said that I was too tall to be good. Now, which way?'

'Straight on over the crossroads, please. It's about a couple of miles along the road towards the frontier, a large, tumbledown farm on both sides of the track. I think it will be safest to go very slowly.'

They set off, the engine rumbling and popping through the holed exhaust. When they had covered about half a mile, Fairfax said, 'Could you stop here for a moment and turn the engine off so that we can hear any sounds of pursuit?'

She pulled up and Fairfax got out carefully, dowsing the courtesy light as he did so. Mountain silence pressed like audible cotton wool around them. The only recognizable sounds came from the valley road 1,500 feet below. He stood pointing the gun up the dark road for several minutes, but everything was silent. Presently the road surface began to gleam fitfully white in the darkness. For a moment, he thought that his eyes were playing up. Then, glancing over his shoulder, he saw that a bright moon was edging up over the hills to the south, He walked back to the car.

'That's a beautiful lover's moon,' he said laconically through Sally's window, 'but no sign of our friend. He must be waiting for us at the top. There's nothing for it but to go on up there.'

He climbed in. Sally moved the car off again, using third gear to keep the noise down. After a couple of kilometres they were at the top crossroads.

'Left here. I want to go straight down to see my farmer friend,' said Fairfax. 'Probably just catch him before he goes to bed. We'll take off at first light. I'd do it now, but there'd be problems with navigation and finding somewhere safe to land.'

The car gathered speed as the rough road went downhill.

'Here, put it in neutral and turn off the engine and lights. That damned exhaust's so noisy.'

In the dark, the car seemed to go faster. Sally peered into the dark shadows out of the moonlight under the wall, hoping that no night-bound peasant was hidden there. The gradient went gently on down. A large, brightly lit building loomed up on the right.

'That's the inn,' said Fairfax. 'I think we might check in there later and get a good night's sleep.'

His voice was neutral.

'Why don't we sleep in the barn where your helicopter is?' asked Sally.

'Because it would seem odd to any Swiss farmer that foreigners who hurtle about the place in expensive cars and aeroplanes should choose to sleep in the hay, wouldn't it?'

'I suppose so.'

'Right, if you'll just park here in this entry, I'll go to the house and knock the old fellow up. I see his upstairs light's still on, so he can't be asleep yet.'

'Before you do, for God's sake put on this yard coat and cap. He may have heard a description of you on the radio by now.'

Obediently, Fairfax pulled on the short blue coat and rather weird little corduroy cap. Far too small, it sat on top of his big dark head. He knocked on the door, several times. Finally the upstairs window opened a crack and a quavering Italian voice shouted down to know who was there.

'I left my helicopter here this morning,' Fairfax shouted back in French. 'I'd like to get some luggage from it now, and also to tell you that I want to start at about four tomorrow at first light, leaving our car in the barn with you for a few weeks.'

'*Va bene.* You can go into the barn, it's not locked. Don't smoke in there, will you?' The window slammed shut.

'Polite bastard,' said Fairfax. 'So that's all the service I get for my hundred francs – the place isn't even locked. Bring the car a bit nearer, please, we'll transfer some of the luggage ready for the morning.'

Sally moved the car up to the towering doors of the stone barn. An Alsatian began to bark round the back, a deep, sinister sound accompanied by a clatter of chain as it pulled frantically against its collar. Shining through the opening at the back of the building, the car's lights picked up the gleaming shape of the Alouette as Fairfax creaked back one of the massive oak doors. The aircraft did not look as if it had been touched. Fairfax hoisted himself into the cockpit through the sliding door. Everything was in its place. Feeling in the map pocket under the instrument panel, he took out the leather cover holding the passport that he had taken only that morning from the dead Jaguar driver. Sally was collecting her things in the Alfa's luggage space, leaning in over the folded seat, when he got back to the car.

'Here, have a look at the passport I told you about. Perhaps it'll give you some clue that it didn't give me.'

She backed out of the car door and took the folder while he held the torch for her to look, opening it up to pull out the passport, at the same time peering inside the flap and saying, 'Let's just make sure that—' She got no further.

Fairfax had a momentary glimpse of movement out of his left eye, then a heavy stick crashed down on the top of his head. By rights the blow should have staved in his skull, but the layers of corduroy in the absurd little cap Sally had lent him absorbed much of the impact. He staggered, swayed and plunged blindly towards the dim figure of his assailant. Sally sprang back beyond the car, pushing the passport wallet into the top of her trousers. His assailant struck again at Fairfax, the stick thumping across his well-covered shoulders. Then Fairfax was round the man's knees, his 190 pounds of muscle sending him crashing to the ground.

In the confusion Fairfax had forgotten about the big pistol rammed into the front of his jacket. Now, as they thrashed to and fro on the stony path, he remembered it. But the other man was quick and strong, and Fairfax's borrowed coat made it difficult to get a hand inside. Suddenly the man jerked up with his knee as they lay grappling. The blow hit Fairfax harmlessly on the thigh but he cried out and doubled up theatrically.

The other man, thinking the fight was over, let go and scrambled to his feet. In the second of respite, Fairfax had the gun out, flicked off the safety catch and pointed at the man's chest shouting, '*Haut les mains!*' The man made no move to comply.

Getting up, Fairfax moved a pace forward, lashing out a left-handed blow for the solar plexus. His fist just connected sufficiently to wind him. Slowly the man's hands went up as he gasped painfully for breath. Sally picked up the fallen torch and came across to shine the light in the man's face. It was the same one who had got into the car earlier.

'Do you think he's alone?' asked Sally, glancing anxiously around in the still darkness.

'No, I am not alone,' he said, speaking with difficulty, 'I have telephoned my friends, and they will be here any minute.'

'Oh, so you do speak English after all,' said Fairfax. 'Well, what shall we do with him? Kill him?'

'I've got a better idea,' said Sally. Then, dropping her voice to a whisper. she said, 'There's a bottle of barbiturates in my sponge bag.

Why don't we force six capsules down him and leave him snoring quietly somewhere for twenty-four hours?'

'What an original idea. I'll tie his hands, then we'll see what we can do. Have you got any string in the car?'

'There's bound to be some in the barn. I'll get it.'

Sally took the torch, tugged open the big door and disappeared inside. Uneasy at the whispered exchange, the man shifted his position. Fairfax moved a wary pace back, then said in French, 'Stand absolutely still, unless you want a knee blown off. Now, I'd like to ask you a few questions. First of all what's that uniform?'

'It's my own, the Swiss Army Reserve.'

'You work at the Allerheiligen Sanatorium. What precisely do you do there?'

'Laboratory test work mostly.'

'What sort of a sanatorium is it?'

'For asthma patients.'

'Why are you taking such an interest in me?'

'Because you are a murderer. It is the duty of every Swiss to preserve order in our country.'

'Self-satisfied bastard. Did Dr Ulicke tell you to find me?'

'I do not know this name.'

'How did you come to be standing on the right road at the right time to catch me?'

'I heard on my car radio that the helicopter murderer had been reported by a hotel to be in Campione. I was stopping every car. The girl lied to me about where she had come from, so I was suspicious.'

'Where did you tell your friends to come?'

'To Monte Genoroso village. It was not my friends I rang, but the police. They will come in hundreds. You will not escape.'

'I've spent twenty years escaping fates worse than death. Don't underestimate me. How did you follow us to the barn?'

'I saw your car go past the inn as I came out after telephoning.'

'Finally, where's my little motorcycle?'

The other man hesitated. Fairfax drew back his bulky fist and gestured threateningly.

'*À vingt pas d'ici, contre le mur,*' he growled.

Sally came back, with some thick binder twine.

'*Mettez vos mains derrière votre dos,*' ordered Fairfax. The man did as he was told and Fairfax, handing the gun to the girl, swiftly bound his hands together.

'We don't want him putting his fingers down his throat, do we? Now, lie down,' he added. The man, looking fearfully from one to the other, got down slowly.

'If you'll get the capsules and some water, I'll have a go at making him swallow them.' Sally opened her bag and took out a bottle of orange capsules, then picked up a small bottle of tonic water from the car's map shelf. Unscrewing the bottle top, she brought it to Fairfax.

'*Vous n'allez pas m'empoisonner?*' asked the prisoner anxiously.

'Only if you don't swallow when you're told,' answered Fairfax harshly. Like a vet dosing a vicious dog, he pulled open the man's mouth and dropped two capsules and a gulp of water in. The other was slow in swallowing so Fairfax pinched his nose roughly. With a spluttering choke, capsules and water vanished. Fairfax repeated the operation twice more, then jerked the patient to his feet again and marched him across the farmyard to a piggery whose open door indicated that it had no occupants. He made him sit, squatted down himself and waited for signs of sleep. It was some minutes before the lids began dipping as the man silently fought against slumber. A minute or two more and his eyes were shut. Fairfax stood up and gave him a stinging slap. The man's eyes did not open, his head merely jerked forward with the force of the blow, then his chin subsided on to his chest again. Fairfax pushed the powerful body, and it collapsed limply back into the deep straw, snoring rhythmically.

Undoing the binder twine now that it had served its purpose, he rejoined Sally, saying, 'It seems to me that the man I have just left in a heavy slumber is a liar. He says he's telephoned to the police from the inn down the road, but I bet it was the sanatorium that he rang. Roughly, he had ten minutes to phone from the time that we found the car until we arrived outside the barn. As far as he knew, we might have gone back down to the valley, since it was by accident only that he saw us passing as he came out into the road again. Therefore, his friends will probably come down tonight as soon as possible and search a large area of this mountain and valley for us, beginning at the bottom and working up.'

'That's pretty logical, I'd say,' she answered, 'so what do you suggest?'

'That we go back to the inn as I said earlier and spend the night there. We've just about got time before it shuts. It'll be the last place that they'll expect to find us since he actually rang from there. We can't risk taking off until the morning, but if we sleep just up there we can be away at first light. And we'll be less in danger with people all round us than alone down here in the barn.'

'What do we do with my poor little car?'

'Hide it in our friend's barn as we agreed with him and just take out the essentials for tonight.'

'All right,' she said. 'If you'll just open the barn doors I'll put the car in.'

Twenty minutes later, the luggage and mini motorcycle packed in the Alouette and the car immobilized, they walked cautiously to the inn. Fairfax had changed into some black jeans, hidden his black leather jerkin, and brushed his thick dark hair over his face in a different style. A noisy group of mountain peasants were singing loudly to an accordion, clustering round their beer mugs on the terrace table, their flushed red faces glowing under the orange festoon lighting. Fairfax stood for a moment by the bar inside, then, when no one came to attend to him, moved into the kitchen to look for the proprietor. A comfortably plump woman in an overall jumped as he padded in silently.

'Sorry', he said in French, 'I didn't mean to frighten you. Have you got a double room for the night, please? We're foreign tourists and have had trouble with our car.'

'*Je vais regarder, monsieur,*' said the woman. She walked to the ledger, hesitated for a moment, then said, 'Yes, we've just got one room left with a big bed. All right?'

'Yes, of course,' said Fairfax quickly, seeing that Sally was about to say something.

'I'm afraid that we don't have basins in the bedrooms, only jugs of hot water in the morning. Will you fill out this arrival form, please? What time would you like breakfast?'

'It will probably be too early for breakfast at four o'clock, thanks. We'll have to go off to get the car as soon as it's light. I'll pay you for the room now. Could we have a bottle of red wine, and some sandwiches and fruit up in the room? We haven't had any dinner.'

'Of course, will Gruyère cheese and peaches do? I'll bring them up in a minute. Here's the key. First floor at the front.'

Fairfax finished the form. He had put Mr and Mrs Barnes of Liverpool in the space for name and address. To his relief, the friendly woman, busy cutting bread for the sandwiches, did not ask to see his passport to check the number he had written down. He paid her for the night, saying that they would have to start at first light. They went up the stairs carrying the food. Fairfax unlocked the door. The room was panelled in raw wood and still felt warm from the June sunshine. A huge brass-knobbed bed stood in the middle, the white eiderdown frothing up a foot high on top of it. A plain white jug stood in its bowl by the window. Fairfax crossed quickly and drew the curtains. Bursts of song floated up from the men below.

'As long as they're still around down there, we won't be in much danger. But we have to face it that there's no easy way of escape if anything happens.'

The girl sat down on the bed, putting her voluminous handbag on the floor.

'The first thing I want to do is to have a look at this passport,' she said, pulling it out of her bag. He sat down beside her, carefully ignoring the scent of her body and the warmth he could feel through his shirt sleeve. She turned to the details on the last page.

'So he was a six foot-odd doctor of medicine, called Peter Ernest Weldon, born in Swansea and aged thirty-five; rather handsome too,' she said. 'What the hell's he doing tangling with international crooks instead of practising respectably in the smoky Welsh valleys? He's been around, too. Look at all the visas in his passport – Turkey, Russia, Pakistan.'

She pushed her hand into the passport folder to make sure it was empty. Her fingers touched something taped to the leather inside. She tore it loose – a small packet of white powder wrapped in polythene, with a red lettered label stuck on it reading in French and German:

DANGER – DO NO TOUCH THIS POWDER WITHOUT GLOVES.

'We'd better get that to an analyst,' said Fairfax. 'He obviously thought it was important, and it's clear from the languages that he picked it up locally.'

'I've had an idea,' said the girl. 'It's clear that you are a seriously wanted man, and it may be difficult for us to find refuge anywhere until some of this business is cleared up. I happen to know a film producer called Stefanopoulos who owns an island in the middle of Lake Maggiore, which is only a few minutes' flying time from here. He's got everything – huge amounts of family money from shipping, machine pistols, scientists, Land Rovers and aircraft. And he's making some spy film at the moment, so he should have plenty of trigger-happy extras.'

'I know of him, although we've never actually met. What an excellent idea,' said Fairfax. 'I can plot a route there which'll take me mostly over mountains. Landing without being seen'll be the only difficulty.'

'I doubt it on that particular island,' said Sally. 'Helicopters full of revoltingly rich film moguls drop in and out all the time. It's the perfect hideout.'

'Lovely. Now let's get to bed,' said Fairfax. Sally looked at him squarely.

'Despite the fact that your life is menaced, and you've spent most of the evening fighting with people, I think you've got sex on your mind once again.'

He grinned, stretched out his long legs comfortably, and said, 'I guess you're right there.'

'Well, I'll be perfectly blunt with you: I know myself quite well. I'm an honest old-fashioned nymphomaniac. If once I start making love, I just go on and on and then have to stay in bed for a minimum of thirty-six hours to recuperate. As indeed do my partners of whom I'm also prone to get distressingly fond. So, I'll thank you not to try anything on. Not, that is, if you want either of us to be in any state to set off tomorrow.'

'Most remarkable reason I ever heard for a rebuff. Are you serious?'

'Of course. Now if you'll excuse me, or even if you won't, I'm going to wash.'

She stripped off her blouse and the black brassiere that was the only clothing underneath, and dashed cold water on her face and small, brown-nippled breasts. Fairfax, fighting with conflicting emotions, watched her with unashamed interest until she had dried herself, got into bed and turned out the light. Then, for some time in the darkness, he lay drinking in her perfume and disturbing female warmth. The struggle to keep his hands to himself was made slightly easier by the fact that his head ached where his assailant had tried to brain him.

Then, to his great surprise, because he thought she was already asleep, he heard her say, 'Are you having a hard time, Fairfax?'

'If you want me to be honest, my God, yes,' he answered with great conviction. What happened next surprised him even more. A small, strong hand landed on his muscular abdomen where his pubic hair began, and slid down to grasp his straining male organ. 'It's big and desperate, isn't it?' she said, like a sympathetic nurse. 'I don't think we can leave it like that or neither of us will get any sleep.' She began gently rolling the foreskin to and fro over the rigid rim of the glans. The tensions generated by the day's events saw to it that in seconds he was on the verge of a ferocious orgasm.

'You're going to make me come,' he gasped, thrusting his pelvis into the air, 'please let me do something for you.'

'Not now, thank you darling, another time. You just concentrate on coming.' A moment later, she collected the torrent of seed that burst out of him neatly in the palm of her hand.

'Thank you so much, that was marvellously unselfish,' he said, and was asleep almost before he finished speaking.

Chapter 4

It seemed dimly to Fairfax that a sudden and excessive drop in temperature had taken place. He felt vaguely round him, then opened one eye. Sally was standing with her back to him, completely naked, a grey V of light visible between her long legs from the window behind. In getting out of bed, she had stripped the duvet off so as to wake him up.

He sat up slowly, mumbling, 'What time is it please?'

'Four a.m. Just getting light. Time to go.'

He got up, spattered some cold water in his face and on to his chest, then pulled on his clothes.

'You're marvellous company,' he said, 'and a human alarm clock on top of knowing even better what a man needs than he does himself.'

'I've had a look outside,' she said. 'There's no one about. It looks very grey and misty which will probably help. I'd love a cup of coffee.'

He gestured helplessly and said, 'I'm afraid that's impossible until we get to your friend's place.'

They checked carefully that they had left nothing in the room, then tiptoed down the uncarpeted stone stairs, opened the heavy oak door and stepped outside. The damp mist promised a fine, hot day, but just now the visibility was no more than 100 yards, and the grass was so dew-spattered that it looked almost as if there had been a frost.

Fairfax stared carefully all round before stepping out of the shadow of the doorway. The mountainside was silent and still. He took Sally's arm and urged her down the road towards the barn. After five minutes' brisk walk, they reached it without incident, and Fairfax began swinging back one of the big doors.

'The Alouette's a bit unwieldy for just the two of us to handle. Fortunately we can start it where it stands,' he said, 'but the most dangerous moment'll come when we crank up the jet engine. It'll make a ghastly noise in this confined space.'

Sally checked that her car was locked, patted it in farewell, and walked out into the yard.

'OK, let's get in and hope for the best,' said Fairfax. He handed Sally up into the cockpit then, with a last look round, climbed in himself. Turning on the fuel and laying the pistol down on the map tray, he began the complex routine for getting the Alouette into the air. Two minutes later, the rotor began to whine round, scattering the farmyard dust beneath the undercarriage. Over the wall behind them, the old farmer appeared half-dressed in the porch of his house, lips moving as he shouted something unintelligible. As soon as Fairfax saw that the Astazou engine temperature had begun to register, he turned up the throttle and the machine lifted off gently. As they rose into the thickening mist, a grey Volkswagen with a stubby aerial on the roof came hurrying down from the crossroads and braked sharply at the farmyard gate.

'I wonder who that is,' said Fairfax. 'Fortunately he's arrived too bloody late.'

He stopped climbing just before losing sight of the ground, and leaned the aircraft westwards, aiming for Lake Maggiore. They crossed the valley in a few minutes, and began skimming the bushy foothills on the other side. There was less mist here. Fairfax glanced round to check the visibility, then noticed for the first time with a start that, half a mile above and behind him, an orange Cessna 172 was flying.

'Someone's following us,' he shouted. 'Don't know how long he's been there. I'll see if I can shake him off.'

He veered off course to the left, dropping closer to the ground so that the bilberry bushes were flashing past just under the rubber tyres. Languidly the Cessna banked in pursuit. Sally turned anxiously in her seat to watch the other aircraft. Fairfax tried a new tack; pulling the throttle right through the EMERGENCY notch, he sent the helicopter whistling skywards, passing only 200 feet in front of the other plane. In half a minute he was up in the cloud, watching his direction indicator to avoid an unwitting change of course while flying blind. For two minutes they pitched and shuddered up through the aerial potholes inside the cloud, then emerged into the glaring sunshine above the shallow layer.

'Beautiful up here so early, isn't it?' said Fairfax, 'but I think I'd better go down a bit and fly through the top layer of the cloud so that we're as invisible as possible when the Cessna comes up here. If that's the later four cylinder one, which I expect it is, it's got about the same top speed as me, so I can only get away by guile. Luckily, I put Maggiore into the GPS as a way point, so we shouldn't get lost.'

They flew on for some minutes without speaking, the little aircraft bucketing through the creamy wisps of cloud.

'Well, the GPS says that we've covered the twenty-five or so miles to Maggiore,' said Fairfax. 'I'll have a cautious look down below.' They sank back into the damp dimness. As the cloud thinned below them, Fairfax slowed the descent and hovered for a moment to get his bearings. There was a lake almost beneath them which looked the right long, narrow shape to be Maggiore. He was about to drop down to just above water level when, about half a mile away and almost at his height, he saw the bright orange glint of the Cessna.

'Damn him, he must have radar of some sort. He probably didn't dare follow me into the cloud, but just trailed me from underneath, knowing that sooner or later I'd have to come down. Now I'm going to fly until I'm almost over your friend's island, then climb straight up, hover until the Cessna begins to worry and comes up to look for us, then drop like a stone and land. My guess is that he'll lose us off the radar for those vital few seconds while we hide the Alouette.'

He flew off at full speed along the bottom of the cloud base. the Cessna following and closing slowly. A tree-covered island loomed up.

'Do you think that's your friend's place?' Fairfax asked. Sally hesitated for a moment, then said, 'Yes, I can see the battlements of his castle.'

'OK, here we go.' Again the helicopter whirred up through the choking cotton wool and into the sunshine, Fairfax taking care to climb as vertically as possible. Even when they were out of the cloud, he flew steadily on up until they were at nearly 8,000 feet. Then he throttled back, hovered and waited. What happened next took him unawares. The Cessna emerged from the cloud, and almost immediately a machine-gun began firing long bursts of tracer out of a side window. Languid green and crimson stripes curled past the helicopter, too close to be comfortable. Fairfax wasted no time. Pushing the stick forward, he dropped like a runaway bomb, although to him even when the rev counter of the rotor had long passed the red line it still seemed as if they were poised for an eternity in front of the machine-gun. Straight into the cloud they fell, a glance back at the last second showing the Cessna turning steeply to follow them down. Unless the other plane made a vertical dive, however, it would inevitably be carried a mile or two away, which would give them valuable moments.

The castle was almost directly beneath them as they came into the clear air. The Alouette dropped the last few hundred feet so fast that it seemed it must end embedded several feet down in the bright green lawn. At the last moment, Fairfax slowed their hurtling fall, the whole airframe creaking its protest. Then the undercarriage thudded heavily down on the grass, and Fairfax began taxiing rapidly in among the cedars and oleander bushes, not stopping until the rotor was scything twigs off the lower branches. Cutting the motor, he pulled back the door. The first noise that met his deafened ears was unexpected. Out over the lawn from hidden loudspeakers, classical music was booming.

Fairfax listened for a moment, then said, 'Bach at five in the morning? Rather cultural, your friend.'

The clatter of the Cessna's engine sounded above the measured rhythm of the piano, getting nearer. Fairfax could see its orange fuselage out over the water, only a few feet up. 'The bastard looks as if he's trying to land. Come on, Sally, hop out and into the bushes,' he said. Picking up her bag, she scrambled out, and they ran together into the shade of a big oleander. The Cessna swept up the lawn and over the house. There were four men in it, one of them with a short Uzi machine-gun still trained out of the window.

'I've just thought,' said Sally, watching the plane disappear, 'that music will mean that it's a party night. There's a heliport at the back of the house. If I know Stefanopoulos it'll be crowded with helicopters, so that our friends up there won't know who's who.'

'Very good. Let's just wait here a little longer, then perhaps you'll introduce me.'

The Bach thundered mathematically on, echoing out across the water. Fairfax stood with his ear cocked, listening for the Cessna's engine. Presently he heard it again. It was still very low, circling in an arc centred on the house. As it flew along the front, one of the upstairs windows crashed open, the twin barrels of a shotgun poked out, followed by the huge curly head and massive naked shoulders of a man. 'Bugger off, ignorant pig,' he shouted in a strong accent. There was a loud bang and a fistful of buckshot whined harmlessly after it. The window slammed shut. The Cessna zigzagged over the garden again, then dwindled to a speck over the lake.

'That was Stefanopoulos,' said Sally, 'in his usual party casting costume, i.e. hirsute nudity.'

'Sounds like a man after my own heart,' grinned Fairfax. He took her arm and they walked across the dew-damp grass to the flight of steps that led up to the front door. A large bell rope hung down on the left. He tugged it and an answering jangle sounded miles away. A short pause, during which the composer changed to Scarlatti, then through the glass panel in the middle of the door they could see a silhouette coming towards them. A moment later, the latch rattled open and a very tall, thin girl of about thirty stood there. She was wearing skin-tight purple slacks and a mandarin-necked orange top. The colourfulness of her clothes spread over into her cerise lips and the luminous green shadows round her gaunt eyes. Swaying slightly, she said in a fluting Mayfair accent, 'Darlings, hello, I'm Myra the Houri. Late, aren't we? The party started seven hours ago. Never mind, there's still some anaesthetic left.'

'I'm Sally Everitt, Sam Hewson's continuity. And this is Fairfax Rhys, known throughout the industry by variants of the seven-letter word 'Fairfax'. He does stunts, rough ones, usually with hardware.'

'Darlings, I adore the grunting stunt men and all that scarred muscle,' said Myra, putting her arm round Fairfax's neck and setting her teeth in mocking fashion, 'and since my lover-boy Stefan is boringly settling down to consume his third starlet of the evening, I've a good mind to ask you to lend him to me for a brisk ten minutes.'

'Have him, by all means,' said Sally amiably, 'I claim no proprietary rights. But if you don't mind we need some help from Stefan rather urgently first.'

'Alas, boys and girls, it's always Stefan they want,' Myra sighed. 'Come on in then. Perhaps we can catch him presently during a brief intermission, as opposed to an intromission. Tell me when you hear the floor stop trembling.'

They moved along the black carpet of the cavernous hall and into the ballroom, which ran the length of the south side. The curtains were still drawn, and the only light came from dim orange bulbs dotted about on the tables. For a moment Fairfax thought they were alone in the stuffy dimness. Then he realized that, apart from the smell of spilt drinks and ageing canapes, he could nose hot, tired people. Shapeless black masses on the sofas and floors resolved slowly into couples. Mysteriously enough, some groups seemed to include three or even four bodies. Occasionally a shadow would twitch a few times before moaning softly and settling down again.

The Scarlatti twittered on, quieter inside but still omnipresent. Myra began pouring out a vodka at the bar which stood along one end of the room.

'Myra poppet,' said Sally, 'I'd really set my heart on a huge cup of coffee. Do you think it would be possible instead of anything more toxic?'

'Why, of course. The servants have all gone to bed, but we can have a go in the kitchen ourselves. Besides, it'll be a nice distraction for me.'

They picked their way back through the somnolent guests. On the way, Fairfax noticed for the first time that what he had taken for a pile of frilly cushions on the way in was actually a fat man dressed in a doublet and hose lying so entwined with a sleeping girl that it was possible to tell their limbs apart only by the massive difference in their circumferences.

'This really looks like the end of a good party, Myra,' he said, 'what are you celebrating?'

'A celebration?' said Myra. 'Oh no darling, this is an audition. Surely you know that the way to a film director's heart lies through his prostate?'

They reached the kitchen. The Gothic vaulting of the ceiling, topping towering pillars in smoky grey stone, contrasted with an array of gleaming white kitchen enamel that would have looked quite in place in a Hilton Hotel.

'Now let's all spread out and beat through the fridges, darlings. Whoever finds milk and coffee first must give out a glad cry,' said Myra. Fairfax opened an insulated white door seven feet high. Litre bottles of sterilized milk stood about on the wire shelves in pale regiments. He picked up a couple, shouted 'Milk-o', and walked across to the table by the window. As he did so, a strange sound caught his ear.

'What the bloody hell's that, Sally?' he said. 'Sounded like a plane throttling back to land.'

The window glass was frosted at the bottom to hide the scullions from view, so he undid the centre catch and edged the two flap sides open. Outside, a weak early morning sun had now broken through the mist, and the light slanting across the lawn gleamed on the fuselage of the Cessna as it touched down right on the lake shore. The wheels furrowed the grass as the brakes came on, and the aircraft came to a halt less than fifty yards from the house.

'Who are those lover boys then?' asked Myra, as two men in anonymous black uniforms backed out of the plane's door and dropped to the ground. A third man sat at the controls, and another bent to stand in the doorway. 'I see they've brought their little machine-guns to the audition,' she added.

'As a matter of fact, they're after Sally and me,' said Fairfax. 'They're the reason why I wanted to see Stefanopoulos. Sally thought he'd be able to help us. I've been framed into some trouble with the Swiss authorities. This may be an official visit.'

'Why, of course, my Stefan'll help you. He hates officials everywhere more than you can possibly imagine. If you'd told me that this was the problem, I'd have prised him off poor little Carole long ago. I'll go and get the guards.' Suddenly serious, she disappeared towards a door into the back part of the garden.

Then, through the crack of window he had left open, Fairfax heard the tremendous voice of Stefanopoulos bellow in its strong Greek accent, 'What do you want, trespassing hogs?'

'We are police officers. We propose to search your house. Kindly open the door,' one of the men replied in English.

'Police officers? You make me laugh. I tell you, get out at once or I personally will piss upon you.'

'You have in the house a man wanted by the Swiss police. He is a murderer and you must give him up.'

'On this island, I am king. You are dung beetles and you bother me. Go away.'

A short silence. It was clear that the men were rather nonplussed by Stefanopoulos's monumental inability to be frightened. They muttered together for a moment, then one of them began to kick at the huge front door with his boot, while the other waved his machine pistol in a vaguely threatening way towards Stefanopoulos. Fairfax tensed with the anticipation that someone was about to get hurt. But the violence did not come from any of the three that he was watching. Suddenly a group of blurred brown shapes raced round the end of the chateau, travelling so fast that it took a moment to recognize them as six large Alsatians, baying furiously. The man with a gun had just time to fire a quick burst, which seemed to go wide, then they were on him. His companion, caught off guard, was seized by the same boot that he was in the act of crashing against the door.

'Seize him boy, bite him,' Stefanopoulos shouted cheerfully from upstairs. The Cessna's engine woke to life with a clattering roar, then it leapt towards the steps so fast that the man in the doorway fell in a heap inside the fuselage. Skilfully the pilot swung the tail so that he was only a wing span from the struggling men. One, blood pouring from a badly bitten hand kicked his way free, staggered to the plane and was dragged in. The other, a jawful of gleaming teeth sunk in his ankle, and roaring with anger and pain, could not free himself long enough to get the few yards to safety.

Then there was a loud bang and an almost human scream from the dog which held him as it sank twitching to the grass. The man in the Cessna stood with a big Colt automatic smoking in his hand as he aimed it carefully at another dog.

'Drop that gun or I shoot,' bellowed Stefanopoulos, pointing his shotgun down at them. For an answer, the man raised his Colt and fired. Glass from a pane above him tinkled round Stefanopoulos, who fired back a split second later. The smallshot ripped through the light panels of the Cessna, and the gunman staggered, obviously winged. The remaining dogs, terrified by the shooting, had drawn back snarling, and with despairing speed their limping quarry ran to the Cessna and dragged himself in. The pilot revved the engine instantly and, side doors still open, zigzagged away down the lawn as another barrel from Stefanopoulos pattered on the Perspex cabin.

'That bastard shot Brutus, one of our best dogs,' said Myra. 'I've got the aircraft's number, anyway. Bloody hooligans; I hope Stefan gave the whole gang lead poisoning.'

'What bothers me is why they want me so badly,' said Fairfax. 'They look like someone's private army of stormtroopers. I'm afraid they'll be back.'

'Come up and see Stefan,' said Myra. 'At least now he'll have something more interesting on his mind than the reproductive organs of next year's starlets.'

She led them up the great crimson-carpeted staircase, hung with what looked like real El Grecos and Velázquez. On the second floor, they paused outside a door. Inside, someone could be heard crying hysterically.

'God, now what's he done?' said Myra to herself, opening the door. The crying increased in volume. Inside a large room, which was furnished in frothy pink and white, Stefanopoulos stood, massively naked, pulling a ramrod through his gun. On the bed, a four-poster at least seven feet wide, a naked girl lay in a tangle of her own long golden hair. She was rolling from side to side with anguish and sobbing like a wounded animal.

'What the hell have you done to the poor little thing?' demanded Myra angrily.

'Stupid bitch,' answered Stefanopoulos, shrugging his hairy shoulders. 'She was afraid of the bangs. So I tell her: you cannot act for me if you are afraid. There is always shooting in my films. I was going to fire a few more times now to get her used to it.'

'No you damn well don't, you oafish bully. Send her back to her room to get some sleep. We want to talk to you.' Stefanopoulos grinned wolfishly at her in the manner of a man who despised women in general, but enjoys being ordered about by an exceptional one. Then his slanting brown eyes with their yellowish whites caught sight of Sally and Fairfax.

'Ah, we have visitors,' he said. 'Sally Everitt, isn't it? Forgive this,' – he gestured unconcernedly towards the furze bush and swollen equipment on his lower abdomen. 'What can I do for you so early?'

Chapter 5

'What kind of weapon do you like to use then, Fairfax?' asked
Stefanopoulos, gripping his left biceps almost painfully as he
guided him into a small hangar hidden from the house by a growth
of grey-boled stone pines. In the hour since they had met in the
bedroom, the big man, showing no signs of fatigue at all after his
night of satyromania, had shaved and bathed, then dressed in a track
suit of scarlet velvet. Fairfax had sat by telling him as far as he could
what had happened to him.

When he had finished, Stefanopoulos had said, 'If you like to visit
this sanatorium, then I suggest you go in your helicopter. I will lend
you any weapon you like, and also a special long range walkie-talkie.
Someone will listen to you all the time here. If you have trouble, then
I come along with some of my boys in the unit's aircraft.'

Now Fairfax gazed about him. Under the wide corrugated iron
roof stood neat lines of Jeeps, small field guns, Bren-gun carriers, and
racks of every kind of weapon. Belts of ammunition, some blank,
some live, hung in neat swathes from wooden supports on the wall.
A Messerschmitt fighter, dust on its wings, stood in the far corner,
and, in comradely retirement alongside, a Spitfire IX.

'Good God,' said Fairfax, 'you've a better collection here than most
war museums. Do you use all this stuff?'

The Greek grinned. 'From time to time,' he said. 'The demand for war films rises most satisfactorily as the actual event recedes. Me, I hardly saw a shot fired in anger then. Now, it is my bread and butter and we shoot all the time.'

'I like those bazookas,' said Fairfax. 'Do they still work all right?'

'Of course. They are regularly inspected, but in any case, I will change the batteries for new ones.'

He picked up one of the big khaki tubes, snapped the plastic face shield upright and squinted along the sights.

'What sort of bombs do you like – anti-tank, anti-personnel, incendiary?'

'Given that choice, a few of each of the last two, thanks.'

Stefanopoulos picked out five blue and five red-banded ones, then said, 'Now perhaps a Schmeisser machine pistol? They fire much quicker than the others and do not jam. And I recommend one of these little Browning 25's from Liège. Light to carry, but much stopping power.'

'Sounds a good mixture. Are you sure you can spare all these things?'

'I expect the insurance will pay if you lose them,' said the Greek placidly. 'You go alone to this place. no? Is important to be well armed.'

As he spoke, with great familiarity, he loaded the butt of the Browning and piled the magazines for both it and the Schmeisser in a webbing bag. Then he said, 'Come, we go and try them.'

He stuck the bazooka under one arm, the Schmeisser under the other and walked out through a sliding door and down to the lake shore a few yards away. A group of empty whisky bottles stood corked and ready on the landing stage. Stefanopoulos heaved one twenty metres out into the water, then snapped a magazine into the Schmeisser and, after handing the bazooka to Fairfax, he let off a tearing burst of fire. The water foamed, spray danced in the sun, and the bottle sank with a dull crash of glass. The Greek lobbed in another bottle cocking the Browning.

'What about the noise?' said Fairfax. 'I've always found the Italian police very jumpy. Don't they think you're starting a revolution?'

'They come here sometimes,' said the Greek disdainfully, 'but I get the girls to make love to them and we have no trouble. Italian men are not serious, and even too quick to be good lovers.'

He raised his arm, the pistol banged three times, so fast that it was impossible to tell which shot splintered the bottle. 'Right, you try the bazooka. But fire it well out into the lake, the bombs blow into many pieces.'

He slid a missile into the yawning tube and Fairfax raised it on to his shoulder. After he had pulled the trigger, there was a momentary pause, then a roaring wave of yellow heat. The bomb hissed out across the water in a languid arc, then came down in a fountain of spray 300 yards out. Nearly a second later, a dull boom thundered back to them. 'All go, yes, these weapons?' asked the Greek proudly. 'Now I give you a walkie-talkie and we go back to the house for breakfast.'

Inside the hangar again, he picked out two radio sets in stout leather cases, switching them on briefly to check the battery meter.

'These are very powerful,' he said. 'Even in mountain country they will work over a hundred and twenty-five miles. I do not think you go further away than this. I give the other one to Myra. She is very reliable and will listen for you.'

They walked back to the house. Some heat was now coming into the sun, and Fairfax took off his leather jacket and hung it over the sulphurous-smelling end of the bazooka barrel that he was carrying.

'There was something else, by the way,' he said. 'Sally found this sample of white powder in the dead English doctor's passport. It seems possible that it's got something to do with this peculiar saga. Do you know anyone who could analyse it?'

'Hm,' said the Greek, 'we have a chemist in the unit, but he makes mostly explosions. Perhaps he knows someone. Do you have any idea what it is?'

'None at all, apart from the fact that the label indicates that it's dangerous.'

'Give it to me, I see what my chemist can do.'

He put the little packet carefully in his breast pocket. They reached the house. A few grey-faced figures were stumbling about in the corridors, one or two mumbling wanly, 'Morning, Stefan, lovely party.'

One of the other man's bear-like arms round his shoulders, Fairfax found himself guided to the immense banqueting hall of the house. At the main table, Myra and Sally were sitting drinking coffee and eating flaky croissants with black cherry jam.

'You shouldn't come in here with that bloody arsenal, Stefan, you might frighten a semi-conscious guest,' said Myra. 'You look like a gentleman, Fairfax, couldn't you stop him?'

Fairfax grinned. 'No to both suggestions, I'm afraid.'

'Well, what are we going to do next?' said Sally interestedly.

'I'm going to navigate myself over to this sanatorium in the Alouette. Alone.'

'Why can't I come with you? Do you mean to say that Mrs Pankhurst died in vain?'

'In this instance, yes. It doesn't much matter if I get killed, I'm getting a bit past it anyway, but I think it'd be sad for Sam Hewson to have to look for another continuity.'

'Look,' said the girl, 'I'm coming. Or else you're not going.'

'OK, OK,' said Fairfax, holding up his hands in mock surrender. 'I capitulate. Let's go as soon as you've finished.'

'I bring you a walkie-talkie radio set, Myra,' said Stefanopoulos. 'I like you to listen, say, every hour on the hour for five minutes for Fairfax. All right?'

'Of course, lover boy. As long as you promise not to drown what he says with your rutting bellows.'

The Greek snorted and said nothing as he sat down astride a chair and wrapped a huge hand round a breakfast cup of green Florentine china. Then he asked, 'What are you going to do when you get there. my friend?'

'Ideally I'd like to kidnap Ulicke, I suppose, but really I feel that something so fishy is going on up there that as soon as I've seen what they're at, the Swiss Government'll be only too glad to admit that I'm innocent and arrest the lot.'

'Pretty vague, huh?' said the Greek.

Just then, a Frenchman, whose face Fairfax had often seen in films, came up and spoke to Stefanopoulos. 'When do we start filming today, maestro?' he asked.

Stefanopoulos glanced at the heavy black lines under the actor's eyes and the sweaty sheen on the skin of his face. and answered, 'No camera could look at you closer than fifty metres, my friend, you look like the death heated up. Today I do close-ups of the fight sequences. We begin at eleven.'

The Frenchman raised his hand in a wordlessly tired salute and shuffled off. Fairfax finished his coffee and stood up.

'I help you carry the guns out,' said Stefanopoulos, picking up the bazooka from under the table. 'By the way, how are you off for petrol?'

'Good Lord, I'd forgotten that. I'd think it'll be rather low.'

'Well, if you like to just hop over the house, we can fill you up from the bowser in the car-park.'

'Marvellous. Thanks. But are you sure that you've got Alouette jet fuel?'

'Of course, we have everything here.'

They reached the Alouette. The Greek looked appraisingly at the proximity of the oleander bushes to the big rotor, then said, 'We push the thing out a few yards. I like my bushes.' The heavy little aircraft rolled slowly across the grass as the two big men leaned on its fuselage. Then Fairfax helped Sally in and climbed in after her.

'No room for me, huh?' said the Greek. 'Never mind, I walk through the house and see you the other side.'

Fairfax worked methodically through the starting routine, let the rotor turn for a couple of minutes to make sure that it would not stall, then took off slowly and pulled over the grey roof and tall, twisted, yellow chimney pots. Stefanopoulos already had the pump running on the bowser as they came gently down beside it on the macadam. In five minutes the fuel gauge showed that the tanks were full. The big Greek leaned through the door of the helicopter and kissed Sally twice on the mouth with manifest relish, saying, 'Don't do anything stupid, beautiful.'

Then he clapped Fairfax resoundingly on the back and waved them away.

Fairfax listened to the note of the engine for a moment, decided that it sounded healthy, opened the throttle and lifted off. 'I'm going to fly at nought feet all the way that the pylons will let me,' he said. 'That way I'll only be visible for a mile or two from the air, and it should be impossible to pick us up on any radar. I've marked our route in on the flight map and punched it into the GPS. First we follow the northern coast of Lake Maggiore nearly until we get to Locarno, turn-ing north after we get into Switzerland near Ascona, to follow the River Maggia for miles until we get to Lake Sambucco, just under the Gotthard. Then we have to grope our way round a mountain called Rotondo, and come out on the western slopes of a ten thousand foot mountain called, I think the Muttenhörner. I see that there is an artillery range there, so we'll have to be a bit cautious. In the valley below we have the young River Rhône, and Stefan says that the sana-torium is high on the southern slopes. Apparently, the building forms a square in a pinewood clearing some way down the Muttenhörner which towers over Gletsch itself.'

Fairfax sent the helicopter bucking along at nearly 100 knots in the rising thermals of the now hot air, keeping the north coast of the lake about a mile away to his left. He could see the peaceful tourist traffic pouring along the road between Intra and Locarno. Probably everyone down there with a car radio working knew that a manhunt was on for a murderer in a helicopter. He hoped that no busybody would report seeing the little Alouette flashing along like a dragonfly just above the water. He glanced at the instruments. Everything normal. At this altitude – no more than twenty feet – you could not take any risks. If something seized or failed, they would be in the lake in split seconds.

'What can I best do,' asked Sally, 'keep a look out behind?'

'All round if you don't mind,' he answered. 'I've got plenty to keep me busy with the map and the instruments.'

She swung in her seat, looking out through the tinted Perspex. There was no sign of any pursuit, or of another aircraft in the sky. Fairfax throttled back. 'That's Locarno coming up ahead,' he said. 'It'd be too risky to go through the suburbs, so I'm going to do some villa hopping up here into the next valley, crossing just below Ascona, as I said.'

He swung the little helicopter north, streaking between two cypresses in a line just off the shore.

'I think this is the most exciting thing I ever did,' said Sally, shouting above the increased roar of the engine as they climbed to pass over the wooded hill beneath them. 'And to think that I always thought that the best thing in this life was making love.'

'I'd say that the two are acceptable alternatives,' Fairfax answered back.

A pylon loomed up unexpectedly. He wrenched back the stick and the whole structure of the Alouette groaned as they just cleared it.

'Don't get over-confident,' said Sally. 'I remember that death is nature's way of telling us to slow down.'

They dropped into the valley beyond. Sally, half-turned in her seat, was suddenly immobile.

'There's a plane coming up fast behind us,' she said. 'I can't see what it is.'

Lifting the stick to give himself a little leeway, Fairfax glanced back quickly.

'Looks like a Swiss Air Force jet,' he said. 'I can't imagine that he's after us. Anyway, he couldn't possibly follow us. He can't go slower than four hundred knots.'

A thousand feet above them, the jet raced overhead, disappearing northward without any indication that it had seen them. They flew on up the Maggia valley. From the map, Fairfax had not been prepared for quite so many houses and people. He flew along just above the boiling, khaki-coloured river, swollen with the melted spring snow, and round every bend there seemed to be more stone villages on the bank. Now and then he saw men shading their eyes and staring at them as they roared past, feet away. Sally read his thoughts.

'Someone's going to report you for sure. Even if not as a murderer, it'll be for flying too bloody low.'

'I'm afraid that this is one of the madder things I've ever done,' he answered happily.

At last the villages began to thin out as the mountains on either side got greyer, taller and wilder. Finally, Fairfax slowed. 'There should be a torrent valley going off to the left in a minute or two. It'll take us right up under Mount Basodino. This particular Alouette is the 319B, and has the Astazou engine that's supposed to take it well over ten thousand feet up, so that we should just go over the two moun-tain ranges with quite a bit to spare. But I'm a bit worried about the opposition. If they have radar in their planes, then they've almost certainly got it on the ground as well. Ah, that's the Bavona torrent.'

He leant the stick over, and the aircraft banked to port and sped up a narrower, steeper valley. There were fewer houses here, and the boulder-strewn slopes below, dotted with bilberry bushes and heather, looked as inhospitable as a crater on the moon.

Abruptly, a large bird flew out of a crag alongside. Fairfax jinked to avoid it, and they passed a few feet away. The size of an elongated barnyard fowl, it stared at them with a beady, golden eye.

'Damn buzzards, I'll have to watch out for them. One of those in the rotor and it would be curtains,' he said.

Chapter 6

Nearly at its ceiling altitude, the rotor of the Alouette thrashed around at top speed in the thin air to breast the 10,000 foot summit of the Muttenhörner.

'We can't hover up here unfortunately, because we're too far out of what's called ground effect. So we'll just have to go straight down and hope for the best.'

Now the vast valley carved out by the river spread out below them. Above it at the far north eastern end, was the blue-white mass of the Rhône glacier, poised above the town of Gletsch. To their left, the valley faded away into the purple distance, dropping away towards Brig and the beginning of the Simplon. He slowed the Alouette as much as he dared in the thin air. They were still way above the tree-line, and it felt very exposed, silhouetted against the midday sun that hung in the sky behind them.

'Can you see anything of the sanatorium, Sally? It should be somewhere in that mass of trees about a couple of miles this side of Gletsch.' The girl leaned forward in her seat to scan the valley through the thick Perspex blister at the front. They dropped lower, crossing the first few stunted firs, standing like grey-boned skeletons among the boulders.

'There are some buildings down there – a sort of compound—' she began to say.

At that moment, Fairfax had a momentary view of something black hurtling towards them, then there was a stunning flash and explosion just above. The Alouette lurched violently and started to fall. The tough plastic round them was abruptly holed in a dozen places, and the cold air came screaming in. Something had struck Fairfax a tingling blow on his left shoulder, and he saw to his horror that Sally had fallen limply against her seat belt, apparently lifeless. Half stunned, he was about to bend to look after her, when he saw a plantation of trees looming towards him at a crazy angle. Tugging the throttle wide open, he flung back the stick. As the revs of the turbine motor went roaring up, the whole aircraft juddered with a destructive vibration.

Either the motor's been damaged or the rotor's bent, he thought. The little machine lifted a gallant few feet, then there was a loud crack and it suddenly began to swing down towards the treetops. He could see that part of one of the rotor blades, half-severed by some kind of missile, had flown off. In seconds, the cabin of the helicopter crashed into the heavy foliage beneath them, the impact cushioned by breaking branches. The rotor slashed into the upper trunks of the trees with a frightening noise until the other blades broke off. Thrown forward against the flimsy dashboard despite his seat belt, Fairfax felt for the ignition switch as the note of the motor, freed from all air resistance, became a chattering scream. He clicked it off, and the turbine noise dropped to a diminishing moan. The cabin seemed to be falling for a long time. At last, ripping off ever thicker branches as it got lower, it came to a stop upside down and jammed firmly between two tree boles.

Held head down by his harness, Fairfax remained motionless for a moment. Then, thinking of fire and despite the pain in his arm, he undid the quick release of his belt and lowered himself on to the cabin roof. It made a cracking sound, but held nevertheless. He undid the girl's belt, taking her weight with his right arm as he did so, then lowered her so that she was supported round his powerful neck. He put his ear to the flat space just under her left breast and heard, with infinite relief, her heart thumping strongly.

Both the doors were held shut by the trees, but the Perspex panel could still swing freely open. Taking care to walk with his double weight only on the strengthened parts of the blister, he kicked the fastening undone and brought his heel down to punch out what was left of the panel. It swung down freely on its hinges, leaving a space two feet square through which to climb.

Gently, he laid the girl alongside the trap, then sat on its lip and swung his legs down. In the sudden gloom of the wood it was quite difficult to see the steeply sloping ground, but it looked as if it was only about four feet below him. He wondered where the men were who had shot him down. Slowly easing the girl out of the hole, grimacing with the pain in his shoulder as he did so, he was conscious of presenting an unmissable target to any enemy. Clutching at tree trunks to steady himself, he carried her thirty yards away to a hollow between two boulders, then laid her carefully on the thick ferns that grew there. He felt her long legs from groin to ankle, but neither in them nor in her arms could he find any sign of a wound or break. He ran his palm over her skull, stopping when he felt a lump the size of a kneecap at the back. She must have been thrown against one of the many projections inside the cabin.

'Poor little girl, I hope no permanent damage has been done,' he murmured, stroking her pale, expressionless face. With an emotion that he hardly recognized in his offhand, unsentimental self, he bent to hold her slim young body against his for a moment.

Then a cracking branch, signal that the remains of the Alouette were settling further down, reminded him where he was. He released her and stood up quickly. There might still be a fire, and the radio and weapons, not to mention the map, were still in there. On the way back, he pulled open his jacket and looked at his left shoulder under

73

his shirt. A splinter had gashed the skin and seemingly chipped the bone. Used as he was to seeing bloody holes in himself, it did not look like damage that a few stitches couldn't repair.

When he got back to the Alouette, he stood for a moment in the mountain silence and listened. There was no sound at all from any direction, only the nervous tapping of some oil or fuel dripping inside the engine casing. He was glad that the fuel was kerosene, otherwise he would almost certainly have been a human torch by now. He levered himself into the cabin again. The bazooka and its bombs were easy to find, the case of the latter punctured by a few flying splinters. The Schmeisser was hooked by its strap behind one of the seats. But the Browning had disappeared. He felt around in the dimness for the little weapon. It had lain on the oddments tray. At last he found it, jammed under one of the foot pedals. It seemed undamaged.

He climbed out again. As he did so, he heard a noise which puzzled him for a moment. That was it: the baying of dogs. Tracker ones. They sounded about half a mile away, their gobbling barks echoing faintly towards him. There might not be much danger from them. They had never smelt their quarry, there was no wind among the trees, and no spoor to follow. Nevertheless, he would have to be much quieter and more careful than if he was only dealing with human beings.

He stood for a moment in indecision, glancing at his watch. It was twenty to eleven. Myra would not be listening out for him for another twenty minutes. He couldn't be sure anyway that the set had survived the crash undamaged, or that the signal would carry from such a rough piece of country. Staggering across the slippery slope with his load, he put down the radio and little Browning on the rock beside Sally. The dogs seemed to be working slowly towards him, although with echoes of their barks from the surrounding cliffs, it was difficult to be sure. Slinging the Schmeisser over his undamaged shoulder and carrying the bazooka under the same sound arm like a hefty twelve bore he walked fifty yards down the slope to a point where the torn-up root of a storm-damaged tree had left a natural foxhole. Poking the Schmeisser through the grass on the lip of the hole and laying the bazooka, loaded with an anti-personnel bomb, alongside it, he waited in silence. Infinitely slowly, he heard the sounds of a search getting closer. If he had been alone, he would have pulled out of the wood and taken his chance of reaching civilization across the bare slopes of the mountain. As it was, with Sally lying injured behind him, retreat was unthinkable.

The dogs now sounded only about 200 yards away, but well to his left and completely invisible because of the trees. He turned the bazooka in their direction and fingered the safety catch. With so many stout tree trunks between them, the consequences of firing a bomb would simply be an explosion, uncomfortably close – and the pointless revealing of his position. He waited. The animals seemed to have stopped about seventy-five yards away, still moving on a diverging vector. A last series of howling bays then, raggedly, silence. A few rustles, a shadowed glimpse of a moving person or dog here and there. Then nothing. One minute, two minutes ticked by on his watch. Then he heard a sound behind him. Thinking that Sally must have woken, he let go of the bazooka, stood up and turned to climb out of the shallow hole. At that moment there was a sharp crack from behind a tree about ten yards away, and a stinging pain in his chest.

Instinctively he put his hand up to the place. A strange, syringe-like missile stuck here. He clutched it, wrenched it out and threw it away. Then his legs buckled and he collapsed as if pole-axed.

Chapter 7

Consciousness came back to Fairfax so slowly that his first reflex was to think that he was dead. With it came a leaden fatigue, so acute that the thought of unnecessarily moving a limb was intolerable. After a prolonged effort of will, he tried to shift one leg, only to find that it was held by some kind of stirrup. Slowly he realized something else. He was entirely naked except for a light bandage around his shoulder wound. Opening one eye, he tried to see where he was, but the effect of looking up was the same as pointing a camera into the eye of the sun – a white blur.

His legs seemed to be parted at a rather uncomfortable angle. He was just mustering the strength to try and wriggle into a more comfortable position, when suddenly he felt someone take hold of his phallus, lifting it, then laying it down along his left groin. Desperately he tried to see what was happening to him, only to realize that the blaze of light above him came from a huge lamp of the sort that usually hangs above operating tables. He flinched as icy, rubber-clad hands took hold of his scrotum and stretched it down, finally gripping one of his testicles so firmly that it caused him a dull, aching pain. Like most men, he had at the back of his mind an instinctive dread of being castrated, and now, feeling the cold touch of metal on the paper-thin skin of his scrotum, he would have screamed if he could.

Then a man's voice from somewhere a few feet away asked in German, 'The measurements please, Fräulein Schneider.'

There was a short pause, during which the pressure grew unbearable, then a girl's voice answered, 'With some compression, the left one measures thirty millimetres in diameter, whereas the right one is twenty-eight. They are rather above average size.'

'Please give me the figures for the other axis. It will be important to calculate the total volume as usual in order to judge the shrinkage later.'

Again the chill touch of metal, all his reflexes shrieking to trigger off in self-protection despite the drug-induced inertia. 'Like elephants, these damned Englishmen,' said the deep voice. 'One wonders what they do to them at their public schools.'

The girl made no immediate reply, then gave some more figures and added, 'I think he's waking up. I felt his muscles tensing. Should we give him another shot?'

'No, we will be starting the hormone treatment tomorrow, and then it will be important that his metabolism is quite normal. These curarizations affect the liver function very severely.'

A blanket was thrown over him, the light dimmed, and he seemed to be left alone. Slowly the focusing power of his eyes returned, and he was able to see a little of his surroundings. He was alone in what looked like a small hospital operating theatre, bare of furniture except for two white beds with wheels, a metal table heaped with evilly glittering instruments, and the operating table on which he lay. Weakly he tried to sit up, but found that he was held by straps that passed under his arms and over his shoulders. And his arms were firmly pinioned against the side of the bed by more straps. What in hell's name were they going to do to him? Usually a brave, clear-headed man in situations of physical danger, Fairfax had always had the strong man's revulsion for the idea of surgery – it seemed to him grossly unnatural to pay someone large sums to do him a serious therapeutic injury, he lying voluntarily unconscious while his flesh was sliced open. He found himself shuddering uncontrollably with the thought that they were going to mutilate him in some way. What time was it? Peering round, he saw an electric clock over the door showing six o'clock. But was it morning or evening, and how many days had he been unconscious? He seemed to remember being shot at about ten in the morning with a poisoned dart of some sort. After he had fallen face down on the damp earth he had still been conscious enough to feel the muscles in his extremities losing their strength and feeling, his hands going first, followed by his feet, cold and dead as meat on a butcher's slab.

The last thing he had glimpsed was a dark figure standing silently over him, an automatic rifle under his arm. Then, in the painful blackness which followed, he had begun a semi-conscious fight for life, struggling to keep his breathing going against the suffocating weight of his own paralysed chest wall. Finally, total unconsciousness had inched in, but not for long. Dimly he remembered being roughly carried, first by two men, then in a truck of some sort. Someone had stitched his shoulder. Then more injections and total oblivion.

The door opened and a big, dark-haired man in a white coat came in. Seeing that Fairfax was awake, he stood over him to take his pulse, nodded wordlessly, and took out of his pocket what looked like a large, blank-faced stainless steel watch complete with expanding metal strap.

'Can you understand me, Mr Rhys?' he asked with a heavy German accent, pronouncing Fairfax's surname as if it was spelt 'Rhus'.

'Yes,' said Fairfax, speaking with some diffculty.

'Very well,' he said, 'you will be staying here indefinitely and collaborating in some important experiments which we are carrying out. Because we want our subjects to lead as normal lives as possible, you are free to move about the sanatorium as far as the security fence.

I am now going to put this apparatus on your upper arm. It has a flexible bracelet which will accommodate all your usual movements. Inside, there is a little transmitter which tells our control room throughout the day and night exactly where you are. They can, by pressing a switch which sends out a selective radio pulse, give you an injection which will paralyse you. If then you do not receive an antidote within twenty minutes, you will die. And there is a very sensitive alarm mechanism inside which will react immediately and in the same way to any attempt to take the bracelet off. It is impossible, even by the fastest manoeuvre, to lift it from the skin without grave consequences.'

'Thanks,' said Fairfax. 'It sounds like an exciting life from now on. But what have I done to justify being assaulted and imprisoned like this?'

'Very stupidly, you have just interfered in an important scientific experiment which will certainly one day benefit humanity. Because of the blindness of governments and others who still think in a mediaeval fashion, we are compelled to work in secret. You have nearly betrayed us. But we are humane and do not kill unnecessarily. That is why, for the time being, we will allow you to go on living. But in return we expect your unquestioning co-operation.'

'Since, if I understand you correctly, it's my body that you're going to try something out on. I assume that you'll at least let me know what it is.'

'You assume wrongly, Herr Rhys,' said the man stiffly, 'it might affect your reactions if you know what effect we expect.' As he spoke, he pulled off the covering blanket and began to unfasten the straps that held Fairfax in his indignity, adding, 'You are now free in the circumstances that I mentioned. I will have you shown where you are to sleep. Report back to this room for your first injection at nine o'clock tomorrow morning, One more warning: never try to pass a notice anywhere that says *Eingang Verboten*. The consequences of doing so are very distressing.'

His limbs freed, Fairfax sat up carefully. His shoulder wound was sore, but his muscles felt like those of an invalid who had been bedridden for a long time. The big man had gone across and pressed a button. Seconds later a red light came on, and a loudspeaker alongside said, '*Ja, Herr Doktor?*' 'Bring me in a suit of red overalls for Mr Rhys,' he ordered. The door opened and a girl came in. She said nothing as she handed over the rolled bundle of clothing that she was carrying, and hardly gave Fairfax's nakedness a glance. 'Here you are then, put these on,' said the doctor, not without a certain man-to-man friendliness. Fairfax stood up shakily and pulled on the baggy trousers, battle-dress style blouse and black canvas shoes. Once on, the red denim gaped to show a strip of skin at the midriff.

'Not a particularly good fit,' said the man, 'but then most of our subjects here are not as big as you are.'

'Who are they, by the way, and what are they suffering from?' asked Fairfax, hungry for any crumb of information that might tell him what to expect.

'Asthmatics, mostly, and people who have gone a little mad, so that their families are glad to get rid of them. Many come here for life. But I must go. Come, I will show you your living-quarters.'

Fairfax followed him out into the long, narrow corridor. Without windows, it had a shut-in atmosphere as if half underground. They walked about fifty yards, then the doctor stopped at a lift button and pushed it. When the doors opened, Fairfax was motioned in and they whirred up past two other floors. The idea of attacking the man occurred to him. Bracing himself shakily during the few seconds that they were alone, he tried to move round behind him, but before any real opportunity had presented itself, the lift doors clanged open again and they stepped out into another corridor. There was outside light in this one, and through the big windows as they passed, Fairfax glimpsed the white buildings making up the three sides of the compound, and beyond and above them on the north side, a small airfield with a cluster of hangars.

They reached the end of the corridor where the passage turned at right angles to go down the other side of the compound. A door faced them, and the doctor took out a key and unlocked it. As they went through, he said, 'Tomorrow when you come through here for your injection, you must push this bell. When your identity is confirmed on the closed circuit television you will be let through. This is the end of the clinical wing. These are all patients' rooms. Incidentally, you will find a tray of food by your bed. This is your next meal.'

He pushed open one of a row of doors. The little room inside looked quite comfortable, furnished with plain pine furniture and navy-blue curtains. Some plates stood under covers on the bedside table. The window looked out towards the towering black shape of the Muttenhörner, on which an evening Alpenlicht glinted warmly at the right-hand end of the early summer snowfield. Fairfax realized that, in his confused state, he had forgotten an important question: 'What day is it please?' he asked, as the doctor turned to go.

'Wednesday June 28,' he answered. 'We captured you late this morning.' His retreating footsteps sounded down to the end of the corridor, the door shut, and there was silence.

Fairfax felt for a moment like a boy left alone on his first day in a singularly forbidding approved school. There was nothing in his pockets; all the little things like his penknife, pen, wallet and passport had vanished with his clothes, and the absence of these familiar friends increased the solitude. And there was this damned dangerous thing on his arm, which at any time in the day or night could lay him out cold at the whim of some individual that he had never even met.

He stood for a moment by the window in indecision, then swiftly made up his mind and walked out into the corridor again to knock on the door next to his. There was no reply at first, then a voice said shrilly, 'Herein.' Fairfax turned the handle and went in. Cringing back on the pillows at the end of the bed sat a strangely bright-eyed, thin, little man of about thirty. He watched Fairfax fearfully as the latter walked towards him, hand stuck out to shake hands and saying cheerfully in German, 'Guten Tag, mein Freund. I am the prisoner from next door.'

The other made no attempt to take his hand, and Fairfax stopped by the bed feeling rather nonplussed. The man's lips quivered for a moment before he said uncertainly in a falsetto, 'Was wollen Sie mit mir?'

'I just thought I'd introduce myself as a neighbour.'

'I do not dare to trust anyone,' said the other wildly. 'I am being murdered by inches.'

'How long have you been here?' asked Fairfax, hoping to get the conversation on to more normal lines.

'Far too long,' said the man. 'My family brought me here, but I shall be dead long before they come to take me away.' He half-turned in a jerky, hysterical way towards the window, and Fairfax noticed with a shock that, despite a wispy three-day growth of beard on his chin, there appeared to be two well-developed breasts swelling out the man's thin denim blouse, He stood, feeling helplessly uncomfortable as one does in the presence of someone with disabilities so vast and disquieting that normal relations are clearly out of the question.

'I am alone, alone,' said the other in a cracked voice, two huge tears welling up in the corners of his faded blue eyes.

'Well,' said Fairfax uncomfortably, backing towards the door, 'just tell me if I can help you at all.'

He went back to his room and sat down on the bed to gulp eagerly at the now cold hamburger and chips that he found under one of the covers. It felt like the first meal that he had had that week. When he had finished, he lay back on the pillow, suddenly feeling tired and noticing how stiff and aching his body was from the prolonged drugging and lying on the hard stretcher.

It was obvious that some kind of miserable experiments were being carried out by whoever ran the sanatorium on the human wreckage that had come into its care. He was certainly not going to submit to anything lightly. And he was going to escape. Perhaps he could wrench the thing off his arm so swiftly that the mechanism would not have time to react. He explored it gently with his finger ends. Its bevelled shape and the tightness of the bracelet made it difficult to grasp and hazardous to try to manipulate swiftly and violently. Perhaps he could shoot it off. But first he had to get hold of a gun, and anyway it wasn't so easy to fire at an object only half an inch thick and already resting on your skin surface, particularly when it was almost at the back of your own arm.

He wondered how Sally was. She could still be lying up there on the mountain, perhaps with other injuries than just a bang on the head. They did not seem to have found her, although he could not be sure. Perhaps on the other hand she had escaped and was already mobilizing their good friend Stefan to come and look for him.

Chapter 8

Icy cold, Sally sat up slowly, conscious that the damp ground had soaked her right through to her underclothes. It was nearly dark. Her head throbbed intolerably, and her hands were so chilled that at first she thought that they were half-paralysed. Where was she? It was obviously a wood somewhere. Above her, the trees were quite still and windless. She peered about her, eyes already getting used to the gloom, and saw the dark silhouette of the helicopter's battered nacelle, jammed in the lower branches of a tree a few yards away.

She dimly remembered an explosion while they were flying, then a crushing blow on the head. She patted round for her handbag, but found only the small automatic pistol and the walkie-talkie radio set. How had she got to this hollow between the boulders? She could hardly have been thrown this distance from the crash without far more serious injuries. And the gun and radio – both they and she could only have been brought there by Fairfax. So, where was he? There was no sound at all. 'Fairfax!' she called huskily. Her only answer through the still branches was a faint echo. She shouted again. Silence.

'Well, I must find my handbag,' she said out loud with automatic human eagerness for the comfort of a few possessions. Standing up stiffly, looping the strap of the radio over her shoulder, and pushing the automatic into the top of her trousers, she picked her way carefully over to the wreckage of the Alouette. It stank of fuel, but had now subsided so close to the ground that there was little danger of it falling any further. She felt round the outside of the twisted metal and Perspex of the cabin for a way in, moving her hands slowly and carefully so as to avoid the jagged edges. At last she found the frame of the sliding door and pulled herself in through it, suddenly anxious in case she found Fairfax's body inside. Glass from the instruments crunched under her shoes as she moved round the cramped and steeply slanting space.

Logically, her handbag would be at the lowest point. She bent down and patted round in the debris of maps, cushions, straps and loose papers. Finally she found it, and was about to strike the lighter inside when she remembered the smell of fuel and stopped to sniff. It could be paraffin and not petrol, but it was wiser not to risk anything. She recalled that there had been a large torch clipped to the bulkhead. The clip was empty now, but perhaps it, too, was still about somewhere. After five minutes she found it jammed under one of the seat mountings. By its light, she found an old leather flying jacket crumpled in the luggage space, and put it on thankfully. Picking up the map that they had been using, she thrust it into one of her pockets.

An idea occurred to her: the walkie-talkie. Unfortunately, Fairfax hadn't shown her how to use it. She pulled out the telescopic aerial, poking it out through the door into the night air, then twiddled the left-hand knob which, classically, would be the on/off switch. It clicked satisfyingly, but the radio remained silent, without even a crackle. She fiddled with it for a couple of minutes longer, then decided that it must have been damaged in the crash, and put it down inside the aircraft.

Suddenly remembering her GSM telephone in her handbag, she pulled it out and turned it on. The glow of the display showed that there was no network available.

I'll have to find a landline, she thought to herself, that shouldn't be difficult. If she followed the slope of the ground down it must eventually lead into the valley, and the Swiss telephone system was of such omnipresence that there was bound to be one down there to use.

She picked her way out of the wreckage again, beginning to warm a little inside the heavy sheepskin, but wishing that she had worn something more serviceable than her light moccasins. The torch made traversing the rough ground somewhat easier, but even so the loam under the pine needles was so slippery and steep that she fell frequently. When she started there had still been a faint gloom in the sky that was all that was left of the daylight. Now, as she dropped further down towards the valley, even this disappeared and the darkness became so impenetrable that she was obliged to use her torch continually. From time to time she stopped and stood listening in the blackness in case there was any sound that might solve the mystery of why and how Fairfax had disappeared. But no. The silence was almost total, no wind, no rustling of the thin undergrowth, just the faintest echo of the passing of an occasional car on the road far below. Her legs ached with fatigue, and her head throbbed with every step.

Suddenly, after more than a mile, the conifers thinned and there was a low barbed-wire fence. At last she could see a few lights down below. Exhausted, she stood looking down, and, at first, it was not possible to identify whether they were from the sanatorium or from the town of Gletsch. Then the headlights of a car curved down from the pass above the houses, and wound through on its way down the valley towards Brig. She walked on again, making better time now across the rough pasture. Climbing another fence, she found herself on a path, gravel crunching under her feet. It wound down at an easier gradient.

A light gleamed faintly ahead. It came from a rough wooden house which stood on one side of the path, with a barn on the other. She walked on her toes as she came up to it so as not to draw unnecessary attention, but her precaution was vain because a dog began to bark frenziedly outside the barn, chain rattling as it charged to the full extent of its freedom. She stopped. The dog's barking redoubled, and moments later the door of the house crashed open.

'*Wer ist da?*' shouted the small, elderly man who emerged, brandishing a torch. In his collarless shirt and waistcoat, he did not look a sinister figure, and after a moment's reflection, Sally moved towards him into the beam of his light, saying reassuringly in French, '*C'est moi, je suis perdue.*'

The little man backed anxiously towards his own door, screwing up his face without replying until Sally was only a few feet away. Then he said expressionlessly, '*Ah, c'est vous.*' She stopped, conscious that she was probably rather a wild figure – muddy, her clothing torn and soaked, her long hair tangled, and dried blood on her face. Smiling as disarmingly as she could and realizing for the first time that she was desperately hungry and thirsty, she said, 'I have lost my companions and badly need something to eat and drink. Can I buy it from you please?'

The little man's sharp black eyes raked her again, then he turned and stumped in through the door, saying gruffly in French, 'Come in, my wife will look after you.'

Inside, the house smelt of resinous pinewood and buttermilk. It was warm, and the bright electric light hurt her eyes. She followed the man into the big kitchen. The floor was of stone slabs and, although it was June, a wood stove glowed and crackled in the corner.

'It was this young lady who woke the dog,' he said in Swiss German to a comfortable-looking middle-aged woman who sat sewing near the stove. 'She's lost and hungry.'

Smiling kindly, the other woman motioned her to the scrubbed table. 'I'm so sorry to trouble you at this time of night,' said Sally, but abruptly she felt quite terrible, the room swaying and trembling round her, and her sight misting over. The farmer's wife caught her with a plumply strong arm and helped her into a chair, saying the German equivalent of 'There, there, you'll soon be all right', in the comforting manner of mother figures the world over. Sally held her head in her hands, elbows on the table, until the giddiness passed. The old man stood watching her anxiously, while his wife poured some milk into a saucepan and set it on the stove. Then, filling a small glass with schnapps, she brought it to Sally, who sipped it gingerly.

The raw spirit burnt her tongue and seared its way down her gullet.

'Are you from France?' asked the woman, seeing the colour coming back into Sally's cheeks. 'And what happened to your friends?'

She hesitated for a moment, then decided that it was pointless to avoid the truth. 'I was in a helicopter, flying over the Muttenhörner. Something hit us and we crashed. The pilot, my friend, had disappeared when I recovered consciousness.'

'You were flying over the Muttenhörner?' asked the old man incredulously. 'But that was stupid. It is an artillery range. The Swiss Army is always firing up there. It is on all the maps.'

'It wasn't on ours,' said Sally. 'We had no warning at all. Just a tremendous bang and down we went. I was knocked out cold for hours.'

'Yes,' said the old man musingly, 'since they made it a range the valley has changed altogether. Animals do not thrive and the crops do not grow right.'

'It is a disaster for us,' his wife chimed in. 'We cannot get the cattle to breed, so now we are going to move to another farm down near Gruyères. There is no point in staying here.'

She poured the milk into some coffee and set it in front of Sally, expertly slicing a long loaf of bread against her body, and putting out a dish of butter and a plate of wind-cured Grisons ham.

'When did you last eat, *mademoiselle*?' she asked kindly.

89

'Breakfast this morning at about six o'clock – what time is it now please?'

'Nearly ten o'clock.'

'Oh, then I must have been unconscious for quite a few hours,' said Sally.

'And you must certainly have a-a how do you say: *Hirnschütterung* in French?'

'Concussion?' said Sally. 'Quite likely, the way my head aches and throbs.'

'I think you should go to hospital to be checked,' said the woman.

'No, I'm sure that I'll be all right, particularly when I've had some of this delicious food,' answered Sally.

Eagerly she spread some bread and bit into it. The schnapps had made her head worse, but greatly improved her morale. Still eyeing her, the farmer and his wife whispered together for a moment. In their incomprehensible dialect, he said, 'There is nowhere you can go tonight, it is too far to go down to Gletsch and you are in no condition. We will give you a bed for the night, then in the morning we can take you to the sanatorium. It is only three kilometres and there are many clever doctors up there.'

Sally thought to herself that that would be the last place on earth she would go to voluntarily, but was too tired and grateful to raise any objection to the idea of staying the night.

The farmer's wife moved through into what looked like a small sitting-room next door, and began to make up a bed on the sofa. As Sally watched her, a thought came into her exhausted mind, and she asked, 'Please have you a telephone? Tomorrow I should like to call some friends of mine in Italy to tell them what's happened.'

'Yes we have,' said the man, 'but it is far to Italy from here.'

'It's all right, I'll gladly pay you what it costs, of course. It's just that otherwise no one will know where I am, and our friends might worry that we are dead somewhere up on the mountain.'

'Yes, that will be all right,' said the little man, 'but do not worry any more now. You have had a bad experience and need rest.'

'Thanks very much,' said Sally. She finished the last mouthful and stood up carefully to avoid making her head throb.

The farmer's wife was waiting for her in the other room, a bowl of warm water and some clean cloths standing on the table by the comfortable-looking bed she had made up.

'Just sit in the chair for a moment,' she said to Sally, 'and I'll sponge the blood and mud off your face. Then you can sleep as long as you like, we shall not disturb you.'

Sally enjoyed the hurt child's pleasure of a cool, motherly hand repairing the damage, and felt so soothed by it that she had difficulty in keeping awake. Finally the other woman said, 'There, that looks much better. Now if you want it the lavatory is just out in the hall there. I'll leave some milk by your bed in case you wake up thirsty in the night.'

Sally fell out of her clothes and crawled between the pleasantly harsh linen sheets. Even before the other woman had left the room or put out the light, the ache in her head had faded into a dreamless sleep.

She had only the haziest recollection of the hours that followed. Once she noticed it was daylight, and stumbled her way like an automaton to the lavatory. Once the other woman gave her a drink, as one might an exhausted child. The attention made her feel very comfortable and safe.

Chapter 9

A hidden loudspeaker in Fairfax's room suddenly produced a strident bleeping noise, and he struggled on to one elbow, then cursed at the pain and stiffness in his shoulder wound. It was bright daylight through the window, the Alpine sunshine gleaming on the white buildings that made up the quadrangle.

'Mister Rhys,' said a man's voice with a heavy German accent, 'the time is eight thirty in the morning. You will be required for injection at nine. Do not be late.' Fairfax grunted a reply, and the loudspeaker went dead. He was really very afraid. The man in the room next door, assuming that he had once been normal, was a grim indication of the subhuman condition to which Fairfax might be reduced. He felt much stronger than the previous day, despite the ache over his collarbone. Perhaps he could have a go at escaping. He pulled on his denims and peered out into the corridor. There was no sound and apparently no one around. Glancing cautiously about him for the telltale nozzle of closed-circuit television cameras in the ceiling and walls, he hurried down the passage in the opposite direction to the medical block. At the far end there was a lift, which responded by lighting a green arrow when he pushed the button. How far did he have to go before the control room plotted him as behaving abnormally? And what would be the effect on the transmitter if, say, he could find a car to steal? Might the fact of being surrounded by metal and glass cut off not only his signal, but any command to the apparatus to inject him?

The lift reached the ground, and the doors opened. He was in a sort of hall with glass doors opening into a small carpark, and then the road that ran through the sanatorium. Several cars stood outside. He selected an olive-green Mercedes, praying that the driver would have left his keys in the ignition. Then, as he went to go through the door his eye caught a red notice which said:

PATIENTS ARE WARNED NOT TO PASS THIS NOTICE WITHOUT SPECIFIC PERMISSION.

He hesitated. That was presumably a warning that anyone going beyond it would be paralysed. Then, as he stood uncertainly there, he saw a trolley with a number of plates, cups and pieces of cutlery on it. He picked up a table knife. The thin, blunt blade would be the perfect thing to force under the apparatus on his arm, but he would need a mirror to see what he was doing. There had been one in the lift. He went back into it and pressed the button for the fourth floor, which was the highest one shown, then stood sideways on to the mirror and took off his denim top.

The sinister stainless-steel box nestled in the hollow behind the deltoid muscle on his upper arm. He pressed the cold blade of the knife hard against his skin and moved it up towards the edge of the disc, screwing up his courage to thrust it quickly underneath it. He was just about to complete the movement when the lift stopped abruptly at the top floor and the doors opened. Cursing, he shrank into the furthest corner and pressed the button to go down again. There was no time to waste. Taking a deep breath, he jabbed the knife up and under immediately the lift started to move. Then cold fear clutched at his heart. The device lifted off his arm in a split second;

but at the same moment he heard a click and felt a prick in his arm and a burning sensation.

'God, I've bloody well done it now,' he shouted, horrified as the symptoms of weakness and failing eyesight began in seconds just as before. The lift door opened at the ground floor and, with the last of his strength, he leaned against the red button marked ALARM.

It seemed an eternity before anyone answered. Unable to stop himself, he slid down the wall on to the floor, then, as the doors started to shut, crawled into their path to avoid entombment. Fighting for breath now, and with the doors jerking to and fro against his shoulder, he saw a nurse walking in a leisurely fashion out of a door on the far side of the hall. She stood looking down at him for a moment before picking up his denim blouse, catching hold of both his wrists, and dragging him on to the terrazzo flooring out of the way of the door. Feeling as limp and cold as a corpse, he began to long for unconsciousness to deliver him from the appalling, helpless fear of suffocation. The breath sawed in and out of his lungs, which he could hear creaking like old leather bellows. His face was down on the floor and he could feel saliva bubbling out on the cold stone as he fought for breath.

More footsteps came towards him, but now he could no longer raise his head to increase his field of vision. Dimly he heard a male voice that he was too far gone to recognize, instructing someone to help him lift Fairfax on to a stretcher trolley. Roughly, his big limp body was caught up and lowered on to the canvas. Then the voice said, 'I think he's been punished enough now. I will give him the antidote.'

A needle pricked his right arm. Consciousness had almost gone, and a reddish-purple mist swam, infinitely painfully, in front of his eyes. He felt as near death as he had ever been in his life, seconds only off extinction. Then slowly the pain and suffocation began to ease. He heard a whimpering in his own throat, and sluggishly realized that it was all that was left of a reflex of minutes ago to scream in an agony of fear. He began to pant like a dog, and his heart raced as if it would burst out of his chest. At last his sight cleared, and he saw bent over him the face of the doctor who had shown him to his room the night before.

'Very foolish of you, Mr Rhys,' he said. 'When I told you that the device cannot be beaten, I simply stated a fact. Its reaction time is only a few millionths of a second, far faster than the brain can comprehend. Now we will have to keep you under special surveillance as a dangerous patient.' Fairfax did not feel capable of saying anything in reply.

'Take him through to the medical block for his injection,' said the doctor. The nurse who had found Fairfax and an orderly in a white coat stepped forward, and the stretcher moved silently off through a series of double doors, down a long corridor and into a stretcher lift to go up one floor. They arrived in the operating theatre that Fairfax remembered, and the trolley stopped under the light. Sensation was crawling back into Fairfax's hands and feet with a pain like pins and needles. His fingers twitched and trembled, and he felt the necessity to move his legs continually in order to alleviate the pricking discomfort. He realized that the element that frightened him most about the experience that he had just been through was the sudden total disobedience of his body, as if it had become a length of old rubber hose, whereas, in his life up to then, he had always been master of himself even when ill, injured or semi-conscious.

Another white-coated man came into the room. His face was familiar, but it took Fairfax a few seconds to recognize him as the one that he had last seen sleeping like a drugged baby in a pigsty on the Monte Generoso. He came across to the stretcher, and, without hesitation, struck Fairfax a heavy, open-handed blow on both cheeks which almost stunned him.

Despite his weak and shocked state, his immediate impulse was to leap up and hit back, but the other doctor came across and said unemotionally, 'If you mistreat the patients you will shortly find yourself one of them, Herr Kisten. Your recent record does not entitle you to any consideration. Now, first, we must replace the device on Mr Rhys's arm. Please watch him while I do this.'

He took another of the watch-like discs out of the pocket of his white coat, removed the old one and swiftly tightened on the new one. The possibility occurred to Fairfax of trying to struggle, but he saw that the man who had hit him was now pointing a small automatic at his breastbone and decided that it would be suicidal.

'Right. Please take down your trousers and turn on your face. You should not have this injection so soon after a curarization, but that is your own fault.'

Fairfax did as he was told, watching apprehensively as the nurse filled a syringe with a slightly yellow, oily liquid, then advanced on him, laid a cold hand on the upper part of his right buttock, and sank in the needle. The liquid came out slowly as she pushed in the plunger, and Fairfax felt it cold in his gluteal muscle. He could think only of the human wreck in the room next to his.

'What will it do to me?' he grated huskily because his throat was still not clear of the effect of the recent paralysis.

'There will be certain changes,' said the senior of the two men, 'not all of them disagreeable. You will probably feel very well, but less aggressive, much less aggressive.'

He smiled at some secret joke.

'Now I will have you returned to your room. I recommend you to stay in bed for the rest of the day. You have had a severe shock, and there will probably be some initial fatigue from the injection.'

The nurse and the orderly wheeled him away, and in two minutes he was back in the room that he had left only an eventful hour before. The moment the door shut on his retreating escort, Fairfax fumblingly bared his smarting buttock and took off the small square of plaster that covered the spot where the injection had been made. Savagely he squeezed the area round the prick mark, hoping to expel some part of whatever had gone into him. Doing so scarcely hurt him because the spot was in the middle of a livid scar where the mudguard of a motor cycle had carved into him as he crashed. The nerves in the area had never completely knitted together, so that there was no sensation there. A spot of bloody serum emerged from the tiny hole, but nothing more.

He lay down again, trying to think. Sally was probably still free, although on the other hand she might have some internal injuries and still be lying up on the mountain. He did not like that thought. Careful always not to get too fond of his casual contacts, he nevertheless realized that she had already got under his skin in a most unusual way and he was absolutely determined to see her again.

But for the moment he was trapped as effectively as could be imagined. Accustomed as he was to risk and pain, he could not face doing anything that would make that diabolical contrivance on his arm go off a second time. Perhaps he could bribe one of the staff to help him; or find out where the control room was that monitored the armbands and cripple it in some way? Perhaps he could organize the other inmates into a grotesque army – no, the very idea was ludicrous after what he had seen in the room next door. Perhaps the first thing to do was to find out how he was being watched or listened to. Lying on the bed, he slowly quartered the room with his eyes for places where a closed-circuit television camera might be hidden. At first there seemed no real possibility. Then it occurred to him that the heating thermostat was in an odd place, six feet from the floor on the wall by the door. And there was a dark spot in the middle of the roundel on which the temperature figures were painted. He decided to go through a little pantomime.

First he shivered, drawing the thin denim round his shoulders. Then he felt the radiator, mumbling under his breath. Finally, after glancing round the room, he went across to the switch and turned the knurled roundel first one way, then the other, looking myopically at it meanwhile.

He was right. The dark spot in the middle was a bulging wide-angle lens. There must be a miniature camera hidden in the wall; and with a lens of such convexity there would be nowhere in the room safe from view.

Suddenly he felt hungry again. Although a previous meal had been delivered, he thought that finding out how you ordered it in the absence of a room telephone seemed as good an excuse as any for going visiting again. Opening the door, he stepped out into the corridor.

Down at the far end near the lift, a man in a black one-piece uniform sat on a chair against the wall. He was smoking a cigarette, and across his knees lay a large revolver. Obviously the doctor had not been joking about the surveillance. Feigning a nonchalance he did not feel, Fairfax knocked on the door on the opposite side to the one he had tried previously. A faint sound came from inside. To his surprise, the guard made no attempt to stop him from going into the room. The curtains were drawn, and for a moment it was difficult to see anything. Then his eyes became used to the lack of light, and he saw that a still form lay in the bed, one leg suspended in a weighted traction apparatus threaded through a hook in the ceiling. A transistor radio was playing soft classical music. The form on the bed had a helmet of white bandages which left only his eyes, mouth, nose and cheeks free. Fairfax peered at the figure, wondering if it was asleep or drugged. Intelligent dark eyes looked back at him, a hint of pain in the frown around them. Then the figure spoke, in a deep voice with a Welsh accent.

'What can I do for you?' he said.

Taken aback, Fairfax answered, 'I thought I'd just ask you about how one gets something to eat. I've only just arrived here.'

'Just press your bell. A nurse will ask you what you want over the loudspeaker. You're British, aren't you?'

'Yes, so are you, I take it.'

'That's right. You know these rooms are all bugged and on television surveillance? They can't see much in here, however, because I've got the curtains drawn. But be careful what you say.'

'*Ydych chi'n siarad fiaith en tadau?*' asked Fairfax in Welsh. 'I'll bet that the chaps who're listening don't.'

'*Ydw, wrth gwrs,*' answered the other delightedly. 'I'm from Swansea myself originally.'

'How the hell did you get into a state like that?'

'Motor accident. One of the bastards from here forced me off the road when I was trying to get away.'

With sudden comprehension, Fairfax realized why the big nose and large firm mouth of the man's face were so familiar. 'Yes, I saw it. You were driving a yellow E-type Jaguar. I was above you in a helicopter on my way up the Gotthard. As a matter of fact I landed immediately to try and help, but I could swear that you were dead. Not surprising, considering that you must have fallen nearly a hundred feet.'

'Good Lord, so you saw me? I very nearly did die, as it happens. By the time I fell, I was completely limp because the second man in the Porsche shot me with a dart through the window from a few feet away. They got the antidote into me at about the last possible moment.'

The loudspeaker clicked on in the corner of the room, and a voice said, 'We do not know what barbaric language you are speaking, but kindly talk only French, German or English, or we will separate you at once.'

Chapter 10

When Sally awoke, the June sun was pouring into the sitting-room. She still had a headache, but the bruise on her scalp had gone down, and her skull no longer felt so misshapen. She glanced towards the door, then realized that it was the soft-footed entrance of the farmer's wife that had woken her. Seeing that Sally was no longer asleep, she beamed at her kindly and said, '*Savez-vous quelle heure il est?*'

'*Non,*' answered Sally, stretching and yawning. 'My watch was broken in the crash.'

'It's just eight o'clock. You have been in bed for thirty-six hours. I thought that we would just let you sleep. You were very, very tired. Do you feel better?'

'My God,' said Sally, sitting up with a speed that she immediately regretted. 'My friends will all think that I am dead. Could I possibly use the telephone now?'

'Yes, of course. My husband is just finishing with it, then I'll show you where it is.'

Sally had climbed sleepily out of bed before she remembered that she was wearing only her minute black pants. She folded her arms over her breasts so as not to shock the older woman, then asked, 'I thought that I had a sheepskin coat, but it seems to have disappeared.'

'Oh yes, when I came in just now I noticed that it was terribly muddy, so took it away for my husband to clean it for you.'

'How very kind,' said Sally, still not awake enough to notice the flustered way that the other woman bustled out to fetch her coat. After a moment and a brief exchange of voices in the hall, she was back, and Sally wrapped the rough sheepskin round her bare flesh and shuffled into her moccasins before following her back out to the telephone.

'What do I do to get an international call to Italy?' she asked.

'It'll tell you at the beginning of the telephone book.' The farmer's wife opened the first page and squinted at it myopically, saying, 'I am afraid that I can no longer read without my glasses.'

Sally took it from her and noted the numbers that she had to dial for directory enquiries and calls to Italy. Enquiries rapidly gave her the Stefanopoulos number, and she dialled it carefully on the old-fashioned telephone. Then she realized that she did not know where she was. The farmer's wife had disappeared, and she called out loudly, 'Please could you tell me what your name is and the address here so that I can direct my friends to come and fetch me?'

She jumped with momentary alarm when the farmer appeared suddenly from a dark, open doorway a few yards down the hall, and said, 'Yes. My name is Zwicki, Anton; and the address is Haus Edelweiss, Schafbergerweg, Gletsch.'

It was obvious to her that he had been listening there. Just peasant nosiness, she supposed. The number began to ring at the other and. After buzzing half a dozen times, a woman's voice said, '*Pronto*?'

'Could I speak to Myra please?' said Sally in English.

'You are darling,' said the voice at the other end. 'Who's there?'

'It's me, Sally.'

'What?' Myra sounded genuinely concerned and astonished. 'Are you all right? Where are you?'

'I'm over in the Gletsch Valley. The Alouette was shot down and

Fairfax disappeared while I was unconscious.'

'Look,' said Myra, 'I can't talk now for a very good reason. If you're in trouble as I expect, I'll come across immediately and get you out of it. But for God's sake don't tell anybody else where you are, and, in particular, please don't ring here again until I've seen you. Now tell me where to find you?' Sally repeated the details that the farmer had given her, together with the number that she read off the disk on the telephone.

'Thanks very much. Stay inside and keep away from everybody. I'll be there about midday. Goodbye.'

The line clicked dead. Upset in her weak state by the apparent addition of further sinister adversaries, Sally stood for a moment by the telephone, uncertain what to do next. Then the woman reappeared and said kindly, 'I am sure you would like a bath. Please come upstairs.'

'I'll just get my things,' Sally said. Carrying her clothes, still muddy but now dry, she padded through the house after the woman, noticing for the first time the warm, feral smell from the byre alongside. After putting out a towel for her, the woman disappeared downstairs.

The bathroom was surprisingly well-equipped. Sally ran herself a deep bath with the soft brownish tinge of Alpine water, then sank gratefully into it. Surveying her body languidly, she saw for the first time just how many bruises and scratches she had collected without even noticing. In particular, a blue welt ran round her slim abdomen where her seat belt had caught her when she was thrown against it, and her shins were dotted with marks where she had stumbled over branches and rocks on the way down through the wood.

Finally she got out and dried herself slowly and carefully. She was just dusting talcum powder into the cleft between her lean buttocks when she remembered the pistol that she had thrust into the pocket of the sheepskin coat after the crash. She pushed her damp and powdery hand in under the pocket flap to look for it, but there was nothing there.

Just then, there came the sound of an engine climbing the hill from the valley road. It sounded more like a lorry than a car, but she hurried to the window nevertheless and peered out from between the curtains in case it could be Myra. To her surprise, it seemed to be a military Land Rover.

As she watched, inexplicably anxious, the farmer, Zwicki, darted with surprising speed out of the barn opposite and ran waving his arms to meet the newcomers as fast as his old legs could scurry. The vehicle stopped, and she heard the handbrake rasp on. The capped head of a uniformed Swiss gendarme poked out through the window and said something too faint to be heard above the rumble of the free-wheeling engine. Zwicki climbed the step in a self-important way and held out something small and black. It was not possible to see exactly what it was, but from the uniformed man's excited reaction, it seemed to Sally that it could only be her pistol. He must have found it when he took her coat, and, knowing that a helicopter pilot was wanted, he must have called the police.

She felt she owed it to Fairfax to stay free. Who could say where he was, and what danger he was in? Leaving the window still open a crack, she flung on her outer clothes, shut her handbag, dragged on the sheepskin coat and fled out of the room without bothering to pull out the bath plug. Her feet made little sound on the matting of the landing. Somehow she was going to have to get out of the house without being seen by the farmer's wife.

Noticing that the corridor ended in a window at the back, she overshot the head of the stairs and attacked the big iron catch. Obviously it had not been opened for a long time, and she had to hammer it with her palm before it gave. There was no way of knowing how many gendarmes there were in the Land Rover, or whether, if they were looking for her, they would try to surround the house. She'd have to take the risk. She scrambled on to the wide sill, the wooden floor creaking beneath her in a tell-tale way as she took off.

Outside there was a drop of about a dozen feet, but miraculously, straw several feet deep was heaped against the wall preparatory to being forked into the byre next door. Taking a deep breath, holding her handbag to her chest, she ducked out through the window and dropped. Her landing was heavier than she expected, but she fell on her feet and, bending low, ran for the barbed-wire fence that lay between her and the edge of the pinewood about 100 yards away up the slope of the mountain. Still hot from her bath, she found the weight of the sheepskin almost unbearable before she had run half the distance, but although it hampered her as well, she could not bring herself to discard it. The strands of the fence were too close together to scramble through, so she chose a solid-looking post and pulled herself up beside it.

Now she was no longer screened by the house, and with a glance over her shoulder could see the gendarmes' Land Rover stationary in front of it. Two men, one in a grey uniform, were standing by it, but not looking in her direction. She heaved herself up on to the top stand. Then, just as her full weight was on it, the staple holding it pulled out of the dry wood. The wire twanged and staples all down the line creaked deafeningly. Sally fell forward in a heap on the damp grass, lying quite still for a moment with surprise and shock. There was a shout from the road below. She heard it and continued to lie still, hopeful that the mottled brown of the old sheepskin would blend into the background at fifty yards distance. But no. '*Halte, halte,*' a voice shouted. Scrambling up, she shot forward in a crouch towards the wood, gasping for breath in the thin mountain air as the gradient steepened.

'*Halte-là,*' another voice shouted, and she heard hobnailed boots crunching on the gravel road. Then a shot. The bullet whined over her head and clattered through the trees ahead of her. She ran on despairingly, slithering about with her smooth-soled shoes on the dew, her heavy coat hindering every movement. Again a shout, and this time a bullet aimed a good deal nearer, so that it smacked into the earth only a few yards to her right. Should she give herself up? Armed professionals such as those gendarmes would probably catch her effortlessly even if she did successfully reach the woods.

The trees were only ten yards away now. She flung herself forward into the tall ferns that grew profusely under the shadow of the branches, falling flat on her face, so short of air that a purplish haze clouded her sight.

After a few seconds of collapse, she picked herself up again and crawled round to peer through the fronds. One of the policemen was already lumbering up to the fence halfway up the slope behind her, pistol in hand. She crawled swiftly on her hands and knees twenty yards into the trees, then, feeling a little less conspicuous, stood up shakily to run along parallel with the edge of the wood. She had no intention of going higher, or of getting too far away from the road up which Myra must surely come.

The gendarme fired again, apparently at random, into the wood, and she heard the shouts of another man bringing up the rear. She ran another 100 yards, then flung herself down in a dense growth of scrub and lay quite still. She knew that once the policemen reached the trees, they would almost certainly stand listening for a while to decide in which direction she was fleeing. For a moment there was no sound, then a voice shouted in French with a heavy German accent, 'Give yourself up before it is too late.' To underline his words, he fired twice into the wood in different directions. The description of Fairfax that had been circulated had obviously conjured up a picture of a criminal so desperate that even the normally peaceable Swiss police seemed to have become wildly trigger-happy at the mere thought that they were pursuing an accomplice, even if she was only a girl. She heard a few breathless remarks exchanged between the two men as the second arrived, then they crashed together deeper into the wood. Sally waited until they were producing an adequate volume of noise before she set off again on her diverging course. She stopped every few yards to provide for the possibility that they might halt and listen, but finally she ran out of earshot of all sounds of pursuit.

She turned back to the fringe of trees at the edge of the wood and, standing behind the thickest bole available, looked down into the valley. To her alarm she could see clearly over the intervening half-mile of pasture that another Land Rover from the gendarmerie had arrived, and half-a-dozen men were fanning over the fields in her general direction. She ran on and on, now holding the sheepskin coat under her arm, her blouse and loosely hanging hair soaked with sweat. There was a danger that Myra might get up there and be arrested as well, thus involving Stefanopoulos. It was essential to warn her on the way up.

At last she came to a spur of woodland which ran down across the pasture to meet the road on a hairpin bend where it toiled up from the Rhône Valley. Hidden now from the farm by a line of trees, she ran thankfully down the border of the field, dropping exhaustedly at last into the deep summer grass that topped the twelve foot deep excavation in which the road lay. Her heart was still bumping against her ribs like that of a frightened wild animal, and with so much running and falling the headache from her concussion had come back with full force.

An engine roared below her and seconds later, climbing at full bore, another gendarmerie Land Rover shot past. They seemed to be mobilizing men from all over the canton in her honour. Realizing that her limited field of view gave her insufficient time between hearing a motor below and doing anything about stopping it if it should prove to be Myra, she cautiously shifted her position a dozen paces to the left so that she could enfilade the road round the bend. What made it more difficult was that she could have no idea what kind of car the other girl would be driving. It might be anything, and the risks of showing herself prematurely would be very great.

A tractor towing a log transporter chugged up the steep road, crawling round the bend beneath her in a swirling cloud of dust. She lay on in the sun, nervously glancing from time to time back towards the farm. She could no longer see the buildings from where she lay, but the upper part of the field behind was visible. Occasionally she could see tiny figures up there, and flashes of light from field-glasses or polished accoutrements. Her watch was now useless, but the sun was directly overhead, so she presumed that it must be about midday. Assuming that Myra had started at about nine o'clock in the morning it shouldn't take her more than about three to four hours if she came via the motorway at Chiasso, even though at this time of the year Customs there would be besieged by tourists.

She raised herself to peer over the nodding grass heads towards the farm. There was no sign now of any figures in the field above, and only the dot of a man by the Rovers whom she could just see by craning forward. They were obviously having a very serious manhunt up in the woods, and would probably bring up some dogs, or even helicopters, soon.

She looked back down the gleaming gravel of the track, and spotted a slow-moving cloud of dust half a mile away. For some minutes it was impossible to see what sort of vehicle it was. Then, as it crawled nearer, she saw with some alarm that it was a military one, painted, furthermore, in a weird beige of the colour used by the Afrika Korps. It covered another hundred yards, while her fear mounted. Then she laughed out loud as the sun glinted off a big Maltese Cross painted on the flat roof beneath her. It could only be Myra in one of the fleet of film props belonging to Stefanopoulos.

She jumped to her feet with a shout and slithered down the steep bank to land at the dusty roadside just as the small truck forged round the bend.

Chapter 11

A severe-looking nurse brought in the food that Fairfax had rung for. Noticing that she was very pretty despite her frown and pulled-back hair, and thinking that perhaps his normal ability with women could help to get at least one of the staff on his side, he got up and said cheerfully in French, 'Well, what's a beautiful-looking girl like you doing in a place like this?'

'I do not speak French,' she replied coldly in Italian. Fairfax tried again, this time in the halting mixture of Italian and Spanish that had served him as a location lingua franca all around the Mediterranean.

She answered, 'It is forbidden to speak to the prisoners', in a vinegary way and made for the door. But he noticed that she slid him a sly backward glance as she disappeared into the corridor. Given a bit of time, there might be something to be done there.

Sitting down to eat the further dose of hamburger and chips that the cover revealed, a movement out of the window caught his eye. A big twin-engined helicopter was manoeuvring in over the pine trees like an obese dragonfly. Selecting its spot with care, it lowered itself with elegance, shuddering once as its wheels touched the grass. Several people stood round like an unofficial guard of honour. As the rotors slowed and stopped, two men stepped forward and undid the door, and a small group filed out of the fuselage. The distance was too great to recognize anyone, but Fairfax could see that one of the men was very large. They moved quickly to the nearest arm of the sanatorium building and disappeared inside.

That helicopter would be a nice method of escape, thought Fairfax wistfully. It would probably not be much more difficult than the Alouette to fly. He drank his tepid coffee slowly, his mind picking over the problem of the device on his arm like a tongue continuously worrying at a hole in a tooth. It would be interesting to know if the Welshman down the corridor had one on. Surely no captor would dream that it could be necessary to use force to stop a man with a broken skull and leg from escaping? Fairfax stood up, ready to go and ask his new-found friend some more questions, just at the moment when the hidden loudspeakers said, 'Herr Rhys, please report to the lift that you used yesterday. You are required for an interview.'

'Who wants to see me?' he asked truculently.

'That does not concern you. Please come down immediately. We do not want any more unpleasantness.'

Without a further word, he walked out into the corridor and down to the end, resisting the small boy reflex to stick out his tongue as he passed the basilisk eye of the camera hidden in the thermostat. There was no one in the lift, but when he got down to the bottom two orderlies were waiting for him. They formed up on either side and took him through the door that led into a long, ground-level corridor connecting with the other wing.

'Where are we going?' asked Fairfax. They made no reply, so he repeated the question in German, '*Wo gehen wir hin?*' The orderlies, stony-faced, walked silently on beside him. After about a hundred yards they stopped again at another lift, getting in when the sliding doors opened. The machinery whirred and Fairfax watched the indicator lights flicker up to the fourth level. The door opened and they moved into a large ante-room.

'We must stay here until we are called,' said one of the orderlies

112

expressionlessly in German. Faintly, Fairfax could hear the sound of loud voices through the thick door at the far end from where they stood. Something about the loudest of them was familiar, and he stood uncomfortably between the two Swiss puzzling over who it could be. They stood there in silence for ten minutes. Then a buzzer sounded sharply above their heads, and one of the orderlies jerked Fairfax towards the door. He went in, resisting the impulse to lay the man out.

A huge, carved, wooden chair, absurdly like a throne, had its back towards them. Fairfax was led round the front. Beyond, was a small amphitheatre with a semicircular tier of seats focusing in towards, of all incongruous things, a large double bed neatly made up with a gleaming white sheet only. At a long table beside the bed, a dozen people sat, and, presiding in the big chair, was Stefanopoulos. At the sight of him, Fairfax stopped in genuine amazement, disbelief and anger on his face.

Lounging back, Stefanopoulos enjoyed his moment with a chuckle, then said, 'I am sorry that we had to do this to you, Fairfax. I like you, really I do. I hoped we kill you cleanly in the helicopter, but it was a bad shot. So now we make you a guinea pig like the rest.'

'What the hell are you doing to me, you bastard?' said Fairfax angrily, recovering himself.

'I tell you. Is very simple. I am quite sure that all the world's troubles come from too many peoples. Many zoologists say that this is whole cause of aggression. So, since the people refuse to stop breeding, I decide to make them. This white powder, of which you obligingly gave me the only escaped specimen, is a new hormone. It has the property that once it is in the body, it is stored for keeps in the fat. It makes men impotent – believe me, I am very sorry for you – and women sterile. It also makes men much less aggressive – is a very fine tranquillizer. You will see. Very shortly you will feel quite different.'

While he spoke, Fairfax had noticed the big ginger-headed figure sitting rubbing his hands and smiling viciously to the right of Stefanopoulos. It was the man Ulicke, that he had shot with a Very pistol up on the Gotthard.

'So all your helpfulness to me was just play-acting?' asked Fairfax, conscious that the hope of rescue that had buoyed him up had now collapsed in total despair. 'Do you usually go about firing on your own men as you did the other morning?'

Laughing hugely, but his eyes stonily humourless, Stefanopoulos stood up to his full two-metre height.

'I am here today partly to punish those clumsy fools,' he said, obviously offended. 'I finance this enterprise, and my films give me the right to buy guns, aeroplanes and strange chemicals as I like. But I do not come here often because this is not a business I understand, and no one should see me here. But those who attacked me will become eunuchs like you. This will happen to all my enemies.'

'I think you're demented,' said Fairfax. 'You can't collect the whole world in this sanatorium and sterilize them. The worst that you can do won't affect more than a few thousand people.'

'I think not, my friend,' said Stefanopoulos. 'Perhaps you have not noticed the geographical situation of this building. It is not an accident. The Rhône and the Rhine both begin from the glacier here. Our compound is very resistant to being broken down, and very little is enough. Dr Ulicke worked for many years in his laboratory to ensure this. If we drop it in the water at the source here, you will see very surprising results in animals and humans in Germany, France and Switzerland. Also we have many aircraft, and rocket missiles, one of which we used on you. We can employ them to drop just a few kilos in rivers and dams all over the place. It will not be difficult to affect half the population of Europe, you will see.'

'It seems to me quite pointless doing it just in Europe. The worst problem is much further East. What are you going to do about that?' asked Fairfax.

Stefanopoulos smiled. 'A knowledge of history – which I would not necessarily expect a stuntman to possess – will show you that most of the worst aggressions start right here, in the cockpit of the world. But we will not neglect the East. We have our plans for them as well.'

'What about you and these gangster friends of yours? You surely don't expect to escape your own poison?'

'We take the simple precaution of swallowing an anti-hormone pill each day. But I do not propose to answer further questions of yours now. You have been brought here for a purpose: a demonstration – some would call it an exhibition. Many of our guinea pigs here are very sick asthmatics or mentally deficient men, and when they lose their poor manhood no one can tell the difference. Today we will carry out a simple – even enjoyable – test on you, and in one fortnight the same test. The results will surprise you.'

Showing his teeth wolfishly, Stefanopoulos pressed a buzzer on the desk in front of him and sat down again. Almost immediately, the door opened on the other side of the amphitheatre, and a girl came in. It took Fairfax a moment to recognize her as the nurse who had brought his food because now she had let down her dark hair to below her shoulders. And she was completely naked. The shapeless uniform that she had worn before had given no hint of the creamy white smoothness of her body, nor its large, high breasts and surprisingly sculptured waist.

'Undress him,' said Stefanopoulos in Italian, 'and see what he is capable of.' As he spoke, he laid a large Colt menacingly on the table in front of him.

The young woman, without any apparent hesitation or embarrassment, came straight across to Fairfax and began deftly undoing the buttons of his denim blouse. He could smell the sharp musk of her

115

anticipating body, and see in minute detail under the bright lights the rhythmic throbbing of her moistly pink left nipple as her excited heart beat underneath it. Involuntarily his legs began to tremble, and a familiar hardening reflex started at the lower end of his abdomen. The faces of the men at the table grinned towards him in nightmare fashion, and as he glanced from one to the other, he saw sweat breaking out with excitement on Ulicke's brow. The denim blouse was pulled off him, and now he could smell the harsh scent of fear and excitement from under his own armpits.

The girl bent to unfasten his trousers, leaning so far forward that he could see a glossy patch of raven-black hair around the erect sexual purse between her buttocks. He looked away with an effort, hoping in an obscure way to quell an excitation in him that was rapidly becoming frenzied. But the tempting scent of the girl's body was too much for him, and by the time that his trousers dropped away, his phallus was in such an unequivocal state of readiness that he heard a harshly nervous titter from one of the men at the table as it jerked into sight.

Smiling up into his face, pink tongue showing between white teeth, she grasped its tense purple cap in her cool hand and, slipping his foreskin right down on the stiff shaft, put it gently into her mouth. It was no good. Even if an audience of bishops had been watching him forbiddingly, he could not have stopped his next move. Reaching for her throbbing left breast, then her right one, he slid his hands on down to her thighs, pulled her to him, then lifted her effortlessly into the air and sank his bursting shaft into the welcoming pink petals of her moist sex.

Chapter 12

The ancient Mercedes diesel truck skidded to a halt on the loose gravel and Myra jumped out wearing a sand-coloured uniform with a peaked ski-cap.

'Hallo, darling,' she said, 'sorry I was so long but I had to get away without Stefan knowing, so I left my own car on the island. This ancient thing happened to be standing in the mainland vehicle park, so I shoved my hair out of sight, climbed into it, waved to the watchman, and drove off. Downhill it will reach a hair-raising maximum of sixty miles an hour.'

'God, I'm glad to see you,' said Sally, flinging her arms round the other girl's neck. 'Can we please drive off straight away, though? There's a manhunt on for me in the woods up there. The place is crawling with gendarmes.'

'Of course, please get in and I'll turn as rapidly as its appalling lock will let me. '

She wrenched open the passenger door, and Sally climbed into the battered, oily-smelling interior. The engine clattered into life, and Myra deftly reversed on to the verge under the high bank, then rolled away towards the valley, bottom gear whining protestingly.

'So what's new?' asked Myra encouragingly. 'How did you come to get all these strange men after you?'

'The farmer I was staying with must have rung the gendarmerie some time this morning. I think he searched my clothes while I was asleep and found the pistol that was one of the few things that I managed to save from the wreck of the helicopter. He'd probably heard over the radio that there was a desperate couple flying about in the area. They damn nearly caught me – I only got away by jumping out of an upstairs window. Now they're all dashing about in the woods up there, firing their pistols in the most un-Swiss fashion.'

'By the way,' said Myra, 'the reason that I couldn't talk on the phone was that I discovered by accident that Stefan had something to do with the people up at the sanatorium. After you'd gone he telephoned someone called Ulicke and tore him off a tremendous strip about those men who landed on our lawn in a plane. I just caught part of what he was shouting down the blower, but I gathered from it that he'd probably be across at the sanatorium this afternoon to raise hell. The lying bastard.'

'Do you mean to say that he went to all that trouble to give us guns and things just in order to have us shot down?'

'That's right. It's pretty typical of him, making certain that you felt so confident and well backed-up that you would expose yourselves just as you did. He must have laid it all on with Ulicke before I got into my eavesdropping mode. There's nothing like living with an obsessional philanderer for sharpening up your intelligence service.'

'Do you think that he meant Fairfax and me to be killed?'

'Undoubtedly. He's up to something so important up there that he's prepared to go to any lengths to protect it. What happened to Fairfax, by the way?'

'I can only assume that he must have survived the crash because there was no sign of him in the aircraft. And I'm practically certain that he must have carried me out because nobody else was about to do so. But there was no sign of him in the wood. He might have just gone off for some reason, but it doesn't seem very like him. No, my guess is that, if he's not already dead, they've got him shut up in the sanatorium.'

'Well, let's go and have a look at the place. I'm going to fix Stefan if it's the last bloody thing that I do. Humiliating me month after month is one thing, but trying to murder my friends is quite another.'

They whined on down the slope for a few minutes, the old motor sputtering and banging back through the exhaust pipe. Then, as they came to a sharp corner, Myra suddenly said, 'There's a police Land Rover on my tail.'

Sally turned and craned her neck through the cracked and oil-marked back window, then said, 'It's one of the ones from the gendarmerie.' She could see the stiffly upright figures of two uniformed men in the front seats through the cloud of dust between the two vehicles.

'He's flashing his headlights now. Do you think he just wants to get past, or is he trying to make me stop?'

'Let him pass and see. I'll drop down out of sight.' Sally slid round her seat and curled up on the assorted oddments that lay behind on the floor – oilskins, Italian newspapers, wire rope, a black tarpaulin. After taking a corner, Myra edged the truck close in to the rocky wall on her right and slowed down. A hesitation, then the Land Rover swept past. But when it had barely overhauled them, its crimson brake lights flashed on and the driver's hand came out of the window to signal them to stop. Myra paid no attention. The man gestured more peremptorily, and began to open his door to step out. Crashing resolutely down a gear, gripping the cracked bakelite steering wheel until it hurt, Myra ground towards him. As he saw the massive iron bumper feet away, he scrambled back into his cab and tried to move off. But he was too late. The old truck caught the Land Rover's right-hand rear tyre and began to slew the whole vehicle slowly but remorselessly around. Feeling the impact, Sally sat up quickly. She was just in time to see the mud-stained underbelly of the Land Rover swinging up as the heavy little vehicle reached the point of no return, and began to capsize in slow motion over a granite post on the otherwise unprotected lip of the road.

Myra braked sharply, and her truck stopped a few feet from the edge. Suddenly the Land Rover disappeared from view, then a second later there was a rumbling crash as it landed on its roof in a gully a dozen feet down. Sally scrambled out to peer over. For a moment the only sounds to be heard from below were the cracking of distorted body panels and a whirring of gears as the heavy wheels revolved slowly in the air. Then, with a roar of fury, a bald and capless head shot out through the driver's window, accompanied by a frenziedly swivelling arm.

'I think they're OK. Let's get out of here,' she said, jumping back in. Myra reversed back from the edge, and they clattered off down the road.

'Do you know,' she said, smiling tautly, 'I rather enjoyed that. I must have been destined to be a homicidal road-hog.'

'I'm not sure we should have done that. Now we really have got something on our consciences.'

'Rubbish, girl,' Myra said firmly. 'That liverish couple had put us in jail – which I am sure they would have done – Fairfax would be dead for sure, and my perfidious lover-boy would be certain to get away with whatever viciousness he's up to. Let me see now, I saw the turn to the sanatorium somewhere as I drove up. I think it's round the next corner.'

She slowed and cautiously edged the bonnet of the truck round the flaming gorse bushes that grew down the high bank. There was no one about, only a pair of tall metal gates, tightly shut, with a white sign in red letters which read:

Allerheiligen Sanatorium. Durchgang streng verboten. Klingeln und Warten.

'I imagine that the gates have some kind of alarm system on them apart from that bell, so it would be asking for trouble to try and open them. I'll drive on a bit and try to find somewhere to hide the truck. Who knows when we may need transport again rather badly?'

She moved on past, keeping a wary eye in her mirror for the other gendarmerie 'Rovers that were still somewhere behind.

Four hundred yards after the gate, the land levelled out on either side of the rough road. Choosing a place carefully, Myra rattled and bumped across the verge and in among the trees, following a row of them down a gentle downhill slope until the road they had left disappeared from sight behind a screen of branches. Turning at right angles, she stopped the motor.

Except for the ticking of the hot exhaust and the singing of a distant chaffinch it was absolutely silent.

'Aren't you damned hot in that sheepskin?' asked Myra.

'Yes,' answered Sally, 'but I'm also grateful to it for all the thorns and barbed wire that it's saved me from. Why, do you have something better to offer?'

'I brought along a set of dungarees. Just like the ones that I'm wearing myself in case you wanted them.'

'Thanks very much. I'll put them on if they're roughly the right size. My own clothes are ruined anyway, and dungarees are much less conspicuous. However, what I really need is some shoes. If I'd had any idea what Fairfax was letting me in for when we started out I'd have worn gumboots.'

'I can offer you some après-ski fur boots. How about those? I put them in because I thought it might be cold on the Gotthard.'

'Are they size five?'

'Strangely enough, yes.'

'Thanks. How very kind of you.' Sally pulled off her tattered blouse and torn slacks, and slipped the coarse, dun-coloured cotton on her slim body.

Myra, seeing the bruises and scratches on her as she did so, said, 'You poor darling, you have had a rough time. Are you sure you wouldn't rather check into a hotel somewhere and recover, letting me get on with the Angela Brazil stuff?'

Sally smiled at her wanly, saying, 'No, of course not. There is one thing, though, now that you mention it: I've had nothing to eat for ages. Nor to drink, for that matter. Is there anything in the truck?'

'Of course,' said Myra. 'I've got a flask of coffee and a bar or two of that super Swiss chocolate with rum and raisins in it. I'll get them for you.'

She climbed into the cab and rummaged about in the deep layer of debris in the back. She had just handed a steaming cupful to Sally when they heard the sound of an alternating police horn coming rapidly closer, and through the screen of branches could see a blue revolving light flashing.

'Christ, I hope that my tracks off the road aren't too obvious,' said Myra nervously.

They caught a glimpse of another gendarmerie Land Rover charging down the track in a cloud of flying stones, headlights blazing.

'That means that there's still one of their trucks left up there,' said Sally, 'we'll have to watch out for it when we cross the road.'

She pulled on the furry boots and pitched her own damaged moccasins into the back of the lorry.

'Right, if you've finished the coffee, let's go,' said the other girl. They walked cautiously through the trees, Myra leading the way with a gait which was still elegant even in the clumsy, outsize salopettes that she was wearing. They crossed the road and moved on into the fern-grown shadows beyond, until after a few yards they came to a high barbed-wire fence on which hung similar 'No Entry' notices to those which they had already seen on the gate.

Chapter 13

Back in his room, Fairfax lay on the bed in comfortably drowsy lassitude. The nurse was obviously a professional at the game, but, judging by the number of orgasms she had moaned through, her enjoyment was not just play-acting. Indeed, it had been quite difficult for the orderlies to calm her wild-eyed lust when Stefanopoulos, seemingly rather jealously, had tried to break things up by saying that he thought that the point about the patient's current virility had been adequately made.

Fairfax rarely remembered a more athletic encounter, and after the first few minutes of wariness and anxiety under the burning eyes of the audience, he had set about her with a frenzied enthusiasm which, he had to admit, owed something to the pleasure of making an exhibition of himself. Knowing his fellow men, and how much each one secretly feared discovering himself to be sexually inferior to another, he had maliciously simulated even more climaxes than he had really experienced, groaning out a convincing pretence of ecstasy, complete with frenzied twitching movements. As he lay there, it seemed impossible to imagine that the great capacity for sexual enjoyment, which, with his unusual strength and co-ordination were the main planks of his personal identity, might even now be being destroyed by the few drops of hormone that were reacting away in his buttock.

He drowsed on for some time, reflecting on the remarkable way that recent sexual gratification could drive out almost all appreciation of danger and sap the will for doing what he should have been, namely planning to escape. He sat up slowly because of a tell-tale stiffness in his back muscles. It was something to know that Sally was still free – always assuming that she hadn't died from her injuries. Although what even an intelligent and brave girl like her could do against so many well-armed and ruthless men was difficult to see.

He decided to go next door and see his fellow-Welshman. It would be interesting practice to see if he could deceive the unseen television watchers. Drawing the heavy curtains, he switched off the lights. As it was still early, quite a lot of daylight still filtered in round the edge of the window. But it would be much more difficult for a bored monitor with many screens to watch to take in what was happening in the dimness. He got back on his bed and lay there again for a minute or more, then slid to the floor and wormed his way slowly and soundlessly across it.

The loudspeakers made no comment. He reached up for the handle of the door and peered out into the corridor. The chair by the lift was empty for the time being. Fairfax inched the door open, trying to avoid too much light flooding suddenly into his room. Once outside, he moved quickly to Dr Weldon's door and repeated the procedure in reverse. As before, the curtains were drawn inside. Fairfax crept across the floor, keeping low enough to avoid being silhouetted against the brighter surround of the window.

The bedclothes rustled slightly as the man in it turned to watch him silently. When Fairfax lay safely under the shadow of the bed's edge, he whispered as quietly as he could: 'Hallo, boyo, how are you? Feeling a bit better? I thought I'd just see if I could cheat the television set-up.'

'I'll turn my radio on to drown you,' muttered the other, 'but, provided that the operator adjusts the contrast properly, these cameras work astonishingly well in the dim light and I wouldn't rely on their not seeing you.'

'Where are they monitored?' asked Fairfax.

'In a separate building at the far end of this block. If you hang out of the window. you can just see the aerials that they use to control those gadgets that they put on your arms. A lot of trusty thugs work up there, mostly Germans. It's very heavily guarded because every-thing depends on those injection things keeping control of anyone who makes himself a nuisance.'

'I wanted to ask you – did they tie one on you?'

'No. I suppose they reckoned understandably that with a plaster cast on my leg, a fractured skull, and a few other odd breaks, I was adequately immobilized.'

'And are you?'

'Not if I wanted to move badly enough.'

'How did you get away before?'

'No difficulty. I was an employee here – I'm a medical doctor, you know. I got here originally by answering an ad in a most respectable medical journal. I'd been working for some months, thinking that the goings-on were a bit odd even for the private lunatic asylum that it pretended to be, when one day I found out about the hormones. I was in charge of a group of asthma patients in another wing who were being secretly fed with this damned progestogenic hormone. I couldn't understand why they were all complaining of being impo-tent, until one day I caught one of the German doctors mixing the stuff in with some cortisone that they were getting. Finally I managed to pinch some of the powder and make a run for it in someone else's car, but Ulicke came after me and you know the rest. You may even have saved my life – I gather that I'd've burnt in the car if you hadn't pulled me clear. Thanks very much.'

'It's quite OK. Have they started dropping the stuff off around Europe, do you know?'

'They're just about to start on an experimental scale, I believe. But the effluent from the steroid plant has already begun causing problems in the locality.'

Fairfax lay for a moment in the darkness without saying anything. Then he asked, 'Have you got any ideas that might help me to get away?'

'Yes, as it happens I have one, but it's a bit slim. There's a tunnel from this block to the garages a couple of hundred yards away. The cars are kept underground, and it's useful to be able to get through to them in the winter without going out in the snow. That's where I took the car from, of course, persuading Control to open the gates by pretending to be one of the Germans over the telephone system there is from down there. The whole building is wired to operate your curarizing device, and outside they can get you with the radio pulse. But the tunnel isn't wired as far as I know because only the senior staff use it, and each has his own key. The entrance is from the hallway downstairs, a door that looks like a cupboard in the wall. If you could once make it to the garage and into a car, and solve the gate-opening problem, you might make it before they picked you up on a monitor screen again. And anyway a car should be pretty good insulation.'

'Thanks, it's a thought,' said Fairfax. 'What are they saving you up for, by the way?'

'I don't know – and I don't much like to think.'

'I'll get out of your room now. But I'll be back. It's nice to have a friend in these circumstances.'

They gripped hands silently in the darkness. Then Fairfax slithered back to the door and opened it cautiously. To his dismay, the powerful man in the black uniform was back at his post, sitting stiffly upright with his pistol on his knee. Fairfax thought for a moment. There was no obvious contact between the television monitoring arrangements and the guard. So there was no real reason to hide from the latter. He stood up resolutely, keeping himself pressed into the shallow alcove of the door so that the fish lens of the camera could not pick him up. Then, slipping quickly into the passage and saying '*Guten Abend*' nonchalantly to the guard, he walked back to his own room.

Where was he going to get a key to the garage tunnel? He was mentally listing all the people he had met who seemed senior enough to own a key when there came a knock at the door and the nurse he had made love to for forty minutes appeared carrying the tray with his evening meal.

'*Come va, cara mia?*' he said cheerfully.

Somewhat to his surprise, she turned her back on the monitor, winked a big dark eye at him, and whispered softly in Italian, 'That was wonderful today. You are a magnificent man.'

'Can we meet one another again?' Fairfax mumbled the question in his pidgin Italian with his lips carefully closed.

'Yes, see me in the lift on this floor at nine p.m. precisely,' she answered quickly, then disappeared out of the door. It was scarcely credible that the microphone had picked up nothing of the exchange, but there was no sound from the hidden monitors.

Fairfax, feeling that there might at last be a chink in his bondage, began reflectively eating the large plate of ravioli that he found under the insulated cover.

Chapter 14

'It seems to me,' said Sally, 'that the only way to get in there is by climbing one of these trees and dropping in over the wire. Even my laywoman's eye tells me that it wouldn't be healthy to touch the barbed wire. See the insulators that the top strands are held up on? And anyway, if someone goes to this expense to keep people out, it's logical to assume that they've put in an alarm system to tell them if anyone's got in.'

Myra followed her along the grass track that led parallel to the wire until they came to a large pine on their side whose branches hung over the twelve-foot high top strands and into the enclosure beyond. 'Do you think that those flimsy-looking twigs will take our weight?' asked Sally.

'I don't know, but if you'll just bend down and give me a back to start from, I'll soon tell you,' answered the other girl. 'I suppose we could try pinching a gendarmerie Land Rover, or commandeering the postal delivery van. But that would have its problems as well.'

Sally bent down and arched her back to take the other girl's weight. Agilely, Myra stepped up her spine in her now bare feet, shoes tucked in her pocket. She clawed at the rough bark of the pine until she could reach the lowest branch, then scrambled on to it. Sally followed her, embracing the trunk. Without anything much to step on, her arms were barely strong enough to pull her up, and Myra had to lock a hand underneath her armpit to help her. One behind the other they clambered their way up until they reached a substantial-looking branch that cleared the wire by about two feet.

'It looks an awfully long way down,' said Sally. 'For God's sake be careful, Myra; if one of us breaks a leg we really will be in trouble.'

'I hate heights, but I dislike Stefan more,' said Myra, edging out along the branch, holding firmly on to two more above. Taking her weight, they bowed gracefully. When she had cleared the wire by a few feet, she put her shoes on carefully, then released her grip and fell forward. A second later she landed heavily in the soft leaf mould.

'All right?' Sally called down quietly.

'Yes, fine,' said Myra. 'It's quite a drop, but the ground's not hard at all.'

Sally began to edge out along the branch. She had almost got far enough when she caught a slight movement out of the corner of her eye. Silently, a tall man in a black uniform had emerged from the bushes, and now stood behind the unsuspecting Myra, pointing the stumpy end of a small machine-gun in their direction. Sally froze where she stood on the swaying branches. Then he said in German, 'What in hell's name do you two bitches think you're doing?'

Myra whirled round and backed a few involuntary steps. Sally remained looking down, feeling desperately exposed.

Obviously puzzled by them, but with traces of the timelessly jocular manner of a soldier towards young women, the man came and stood beneath the branch she was on and said, 'If you were only wearing a skirt, the view from here would be even better, but I think that you'd better go back outside the wire before you get hurt.' Sally shuffled her feet on the branch as if about to comply.

'Go on, get back,' shouted the man, gesturing with his right arm while he held the weight of the gun in the other. Aiming herself as carefully as she could, she let go of the top branch and dropped into space. The man had a half second in which to avoid her, jumped back, tripped over a small tree stump and crumpled forward so that one of her well-shod feet caught him a thumping blow between the shoulder blades. With a bubbling cry, he lay still.

Sally lay motionless for a moment on top of him. Myra leapt forward and wrenched the gun from the man's limp hand, saying, 'Are you all right, Sally darling? That was a madly brave thing to do. I shall personally call for an OBE for you when we get back to the Queen.'

'God, what a bloody headache I've got now,' moaned Sally. 'Just don't let's do anything while I decide for a moment if I'm going to be sick.' She struggled off her victim and sat on the damp leaf mould, her head between her hands. 'If I had concussion before,' she said, 'my brain must be one vast bruise now.'

The big man groaned and twitched.

'I hoped you'd killed him, you poor angel, but actually I think he's only stunned. Perhaps he can give us some useful information. Let's tie him up.'

She heaved the limp body over so that she could undo his black webbing belt, strip it off, then bind it round his hands and refasten it.

'Do you think he's alone?' said Sally. 'And what kind of uniform is that? If there are any more about built like him, I've half a mind to turn and run.'

'Actually, I was thinking that the first thing we'd better do is to get this oaf to go down to the gate with us and show us how to operate it so as to be sure of our line of retreat. By the way, do you know how these things work?'

She held out the machine-gun. Sally stood up shakily. 'I've fiddled about with quite a few of them over the years,' she said. 'As far as I'm concerned, the first thing's to find the safety catch.'

She ran her hand down the barrel and said, 'This looks like it, and it's obligingly labelled "on" instead of being in Russian or something.

And to cock it, you yank this big knob back into the position it's in now.'

'How efficient you are in this man's world, ducky. Thanks very much,' said Myra admiringly. 'By the way, as I've got this thing now, perhaps you'd like to have the dinky little pearl-handled Browning that Stefan gave me to defend my virtue – as if he cared.'

She pulled the bright toy-sized weapon out of her denim pocket and handed it, butt first, to Sally, adding, 'It's fully loaded, of course.'

The man at their feet moaned again and his eyelids fluttered. 'Get up, you pig. I can see you're only pretending to be dead,' said Myra harshly to him.

After a pause, he croaked in good English, but with a thick accent, 'I-think-my-neck-is-broken.'

'You men are all the same, bloody hypochondriacs. Get up I say,' said Myra, jerking the gun towards him. Painfully, he got to his feet.

'Now you are going to show us how to open the main gate,' said Sally.

'But I cannot do that,' said the man. 'First, it is watched by a television camera on both sides, and secondly, my life will be in danger if I take you down there.'

'No more than our lives are,' said Sally, 'if as much.'

'You are wrong, *mademoiselle*,' said the man earnestly. 'I am not a free agent, but a prisoner here myself. I am a skiing instructor and came here to convalesce after a bad accident. I have a radio-controlled apparatus on my left arm, which my masters track all the time, and which makes it possible for them to stun me anywhere at will. Even now they will know that I have been standing in one place for too long and will be wondering why.'

'You're trying to bluff us,' said Myra coldly, jabbing at the small of the man's back with the machine-gun.

'Please, no, I promise I was a patient here and only became a guard because the alternative was to be made into a guinea-pig on whom new drugs are tried out,' pleaded the man. 'But now we must move towards the gate if we are to avoid someone coming to investigate us.'

They walked off along a narrow track parallel with the wire, the man leading, followed by Myra, and with Sally bringing up the rear. After two minutes, the man stopped and pointed through the trees to the massive white gates about forty yards away.

'You see the pole standing just off the road,' he said in a low voice, 'well, that's the television camera. Then there are microphones in the box on top of the gateposts to catch any noises. The gate is opened electrically from the control centre. There is a switch at the side of the gate in a glass box which can be used in an emergency, but it can also be overruled by the control centre.'

'It looks a jolly solid structure,' said Sally. 'What's it made of?'

'Metal, mostly,' he answered. 'I think it would be proof against anything except a shell.'

'Do you think we can trust him, Myra?' said Sally suddenly.

'As a matter of fact my woman's intuition tells me that we can,' said the other girl. 'I was just wondering whether we could get this thing off his arm and destroy whatever it is. Otherwise we're very restricted in what we can get away with.'

'I have thought of a way,' he said, 'but it is dangerous and also I cannot do it for myself. When the time comes for me to go off duty in about' – he glanced at his watch – 'half an hour, I have to go up past the garage. I believe there is something in there that we can use to get this off without it half-killing me.'

'What do you have to do meanwhile?' asked Sally.

'Patrol the perimeter wire for about a kilometre until I reach my colleague for a rendezvous – I should be there already. Then I go back up to the sanatorium.'

'Is your colleague an ex-prisoner like you?'

'No. He is a German and was in the Hitler Jugend during the war.

135

Very fanatical about the work that is being done here. It would be most dangerous if he saw you with me.'

'What precisely is being done here?' asked Myra.

'The group in charge has a plan to sterilize everyone on earth except themselves and the few people to whom they care to issue special antidote pills. As the hormones will be distributed so widely, they have also had to develop many other plans – for meat substitutes, for example, because flocks of animals will also be sterilized and die out unless they receive the anti-hormones. It is a very grandiose plan. At first I thought they were all harmlessly mad, but now I am not at all sure. But I would like to ask you a question: for whom are you working? The CIA or somebody?'

Sally smiled. 'I'm flattered at being taken for a professional,' she answered. 'No, as a matter of fact, we believe that your masters have taken one of our friends prisoner – perhaps you can confirm to us anyway: he's a powerfully built, black-haired man called Fairfax Rhys.'

'When did they get him, do you know?'

'It must have been a couple of days ago. He and I were in a helicopter that was shot down on the hill a few miles to the south.'

'Ah yes, a number of my colleagues went out with dogs to pick him up. The pilot was not badly hurt, I think. Now they are experimenting on him.'

'Experimenting? How?' said Sally, aghast.

The man did not answer, only stopped abruptly in his tracks, so suddenly that Myra dug him in the back with the gun, just as he turned from the waist holding his finger to his lips. At the same moment they heard someone crashing through the bushes less than fifty yards away. He whispered quickly, 'Please give me back my gun, and hide among the trees. I will meet you back here in ten minutes. I promise.'

Silently Myra handed over the gun and the man moved off, crashing into branches, shuffling his feet and whistling in order to drown the noise the two girls made throwing themselves into cover.

'*Bist Du da, Hans?*' shouted the other man as he approached. 'Is there something wrong?'

'No, why?' Hans answered.

'You're late, that's why. I thought perhaps you'd had some trouble.' Crouching, pistol in hand, behind a tree, Sally tried hard to listen to their further conversation. But once they met it was too faint to understand. Myra leaned against her to make the most of their inadequate cover. They could just see the thick, black-trousered legs of the other man as he stood chatting and smoking a cigarette. The wood was now totally silent all around them. Sally felt the foot she was sitting on going to sleep. Cautiously she tried to move it, but a rustle started from a bramble caught under her boot, and she resigned herself to staying in the same uncomfortable position. She was glad that she had changed into the khaki dungarees. Her own brightly coloured clothes, mud-stained although they had been, would still have been far too visible.

At last the other man finished his cigarette and moved off. Hans waited for a moment while he got out of earshot, then turned to come back to them.

'Do you want my gun back?' he asked Myra. 'I swear that I can be trusted with it. If you help me to escape, I will gladly do anything that you want.'

'All right, you keep it,' said Myra 'So the first thing that we do is to try and get rid of that thing on your arm. Where's this garage?'

'Please follow me, but not closer than twenty-five metres behind because I could easily meet another guard or one of the doctors. If I whistle a tune suddenly, please hide immediately. Now we have no more than twenty minutes for me to get back to my barrack block, so we will have to work fast. They do not usually paralyse guards for being late, but you can never be quite sure. They are deliberately unpredictable so as to ensure instant obedience.'

He set off, walking rapidly up the hill along a narrow earth path that led between the pines. Sally followed him at the distance he had asked, and Myra brought up the rear.

Chapter 15

Fairfax woke from an hour's sleep feeling much refreshed. The sun had set outside and the sky had clouded over and gone the luminous navy-blue of evening. He glanced at his watch: it was nearly 8.40. How did one prepare for an illicit date in a lift with one of one's gaolers? He shaved himself with the tethered electric razor that the sanatorium thoughtfully provided to avoid putting in the hands of its patients a potential means of suicide.

After washing himself, noting in the process that his shoulder was healing with the customary effortlessness that his body always showed, he put on the crumpled denim again. Hardly the sort of thing that one usually wore as mating plumage, but there was no alternative.

Opening the door, he glanced down the passage. The guard was still sitting there. It was now 8.55. Deciding that it would be important for the future of any relationship with the girl, to avoid drawing any suspicion to her, he walked boldly past the man and pressed the button to call the lift.

The guard lifted his great red face towards Fairfax and said expressionlessly, 'Where are you going?'

'Downstairs,' he answered briefly.

'What for?'

'Exercise.' Apparently satisfied by this colourless exchange, the guard said, 'If you are not back within half an hour, you will be paralysed, wherever you are,' then looked down boredly at his watch to check the time.

Fairfax got into the lift and pressed the button to go down to the ground floor. His date could, he supposed, be some kind of ambush, but it hardly seemed likely. The warmth with which the girl had behaved hardly seemed simulated.

The doors opened and he glanced around. The hall was empty and silent, but it was impossible to say what hidden eyes were on him. The door shut again and he stood in the mufffled silence, remembering with a shudder the awful occasion the day before when he had tried to free himself from the curarizing device. His watch – the only survivor of his personal belongings – showed exactly nine o'clock, so he pressed the button for the top floor. The bright landing light flooded in as the door rolled back. For a moment he saw no one, then the girl appeared from a door a few yards down. She was still in her severe grey uniform, but had undone the top two buttons at the front in a symbolic gesture of invitation, and also let down her long black hair. Fingers on her full lips, she signalled him not to say anything, and to follow her, having first sent the lift back to the ground floor.

She led him into a small empty ward, locking the door behind her. The main lights were not on, only a dim reading lamp on a desk in the corner. She put an arm on his shoulder and stood looking at him for a moment, eyes shining in the manner of someone who can scarcely believe her luck.

'I have waited a long time for someone like you up here,' she said in Italian, 'my name is Lydia, and yours I know from your card is Fairfax. I feel that you are considerate, strong and very, very manly. I have tested many patients, but there was never one like you. I could love you a great deal.'

Fairfax, naturally a kind man, tended to be embarrassed by real emotion and warmth. Years of avoiding entanglements that would threaten his way of life had made talk of love affect him like the sound of gunfire on an untrained Labrador. He stifled the reflex to discourage her, and allowed her to pull him to her in an absorbed way. Then she kissed him repeatedly on the cheeks, forehead, and eyes with soft, feverishly dry lips, murmuring in a low voice. He wrapped his arms round her and hugged her body until he felt her large breasts crush against his ribs. But before he kissed her back, he asked cautiously, 'Are you sure that there are no cameras or microphones in here?'

'No, there are not,' she said, her eyes languorous. 'The door is always locked and only the staff have keys.' She reached up behind his head and pulled his face down to meet her, her tongue darting hungrily into his mouth as their lips met. Cold-bloodedly, he thought, if I want to get a key for the tunnel from her, I shall have to choose a moment when it will be impossible for her to refuse. Again he noticed her natural musk, partially overlaid this time by a torrid perfume which she had put lavishly behind her ears and in her hair.

Through the thin material he ran his hand down her spine to the cleft between her buttocks, which tautened together as his hand edged between them. With momentary surprise he felt that she was wearing nothing beneath her overall. Her hands began picking at his shoulders, then swung down his back in caressing arcs, finally moving without hesitation to the bones of his pelvis at the front. They stayed there for a moment, kneading impatiently. Then she moved her fingers, touching him so lightly that it was barely perceptible, across to the quivering shaft of his stiff phallus. She moaned softly as she felt it. Lifting the skirt of her overall, he worked his fingers down her ample buttocks and into the warm division at the bottom. Beneath the hair he found a soft, pulpy humidity which made his heart pound. Her fingers were already fumbling avidly at the crude metal buttons on the fly of his denims, while little noises sounded in her throat. He bent to kiss her hard and long, his fingers immersed now in her welcoming wetness.

'Please, please, please,' she muttered in Italian, pulling him towards an examination couch that stood along the wall, and sinking backwards on to it in the dim light. Quickly he unpicked the front row of buttons on her uniform, and the cloth fell away from her luxurious body. His denim trousers had slid to the floor, and he lifted his feet one by one to jettison them. She lay back, legs invitingly wide apart, eyes shut, mouth open, thighs jerking up with yawning expectation.

'Will you do something for me?' he asked, as he sank purposefully towards her.

'Anything, anything,' she answered, lashing her head from side to side as she felt the very beginning of his hard presence inside her.

'Promise to get me a key to the garage tunnel.' For a second, he thought that he had misjudged his moment. Her body stiffened slightly and her eyelashes flickered as if her trance had been broken. Then she dug her fingers into his muscular buttocks and murmured, 'I promise.'

'Tonight if possible, and if not, without fail, tomorrow,' he said holding himself back with an effort from yielding to the warm suction of the threshold that gripped him.

'Tonight, tonight,' she muttered, trembling and arching her back jerkily to remove the torment of his suspended entry. 'But we will see one another again?'

'Of course,' he said untruthfully, jerking himself in, and feeling his ripe rigidity slither through her well-prepared flesh. Wildly she jerked at his buttocks, desperate to start him into a cumulative rhythm which would slake her hunger with the minimum delay.

It seemed only seconds later that Fairfax, running with sweat and panting for breath looked at his watch and saw that he had been away from his room for twenty-eight minutes. The girl was now more languid beneath him, but when she felt him draw away she said anxiously. 'No, please don't go.'

'I have to,' he answered, 'the guard downstairs warned that they would paralyse me if I was away longer than half an hour.'

She lay for a moment absorbing this news in silence, then said, 'In that case, you must go. I will bring the key to your room later. Men like you are rare. The experience was exquisite both times, but not really long enough.'

'Thank you, my angel,' answered Fairfax, swiftly buttoning on his clothes and smoothing his dishevelled dark hair. She kissed him passionately for a last time, then watched him into the lift with a burning possessiveness in her face as she said, 'If you leave here, I come with you. Life is intolerably lonely up here because we are never even allowed into the village. It is a prison; I need you too much to let you go.'

He felt a pang of real emotion as he left her standing forlornly staring after him, but he knew that, if he was ever to get away from this bizarre prison, he had for once to resist the sumptuous temptation that the girl represented. He got into the lift and, just to deceive the guard, sank down to the ground floor again before going back up to his own floor.

'Hm. You just made it,' said the guard. 'Another minute and I would have rung the control centre to tell them you were missing.' He gestured towards a black telephone on the wall. Fairfax, glad only that his sweat-soaked hair and flushed face had escaped notice, went back to his room without a word.

Chapter 16

'Tell me how many guards have we got on the strength now, Ulicke?' asked Stefanopoulos, as he strode down the corridor towards the control centre.

The heavily built doctor, puffing with the unwelcome exercise, answered, 'There are four hundred in all. Two hundred are trusted men, their records known to us, and the remainder are secured with the device. Thus we have one trusty who is responsible for each prisoner-guard.'

'Do you need more people? We must be near the limit of the amount that the Sick Funds and patients' relatives can pay.'

'The numbers at present are enough for guard work and limited distribution of the hormone. But as these activities are stepped up so we will need perhaps to double the present numbers, particularly when we are working on a worldwide scale. You will remember that we originally thought that it might be necessary to defend the sanatorium against a military strike, but we do not think now that this is a real possibility. Since we discovered that the effects of the hormone are irreversible, unless caught early, we have realized that continuous dosage will not be necessary, which also reduces the manpower needs greatly.'

'I see,' said Stefanopoulos. 'I am also assuming that, as we seriously begin distribution, we will move our stores and aircraft down to my island of Protos. The continual coming and going of helicopters and large twins will attract much less attention in the Aegean than here in Switzerland or Italy. And it will also be much cheaper.'

'Yes,' said Ulicke.

They had reached the rather grim structure of the Control building. Bristling with aerials on the roof, it was built of heavy concrete and windowless on the ground and first two floors. The glass of the top floor was protected with metal grilles. Outside the main door, a guard stood in a bullet-proof glass box with an electronic control panel in front of him, his sub-machine-gun held barrel down, in front of him. When he saw Ulicke, he came smartly to attention and barked out, '*Guten Tag, Herr Doktor*', through the voice louvre and pressed a button which slid back a heavy metal door in the concrete wall.

Ducking his head under the door arch, despite its two metres height, Stefanopoulos led the way in, saying, 'Once anyone has got through this door, what is to stop them getting into the control room?'

'Many things,' answered Ulicke. 'First of all this whole ante-room floor is electroconductive and can be electrified with five thousand volts. Secondly, the lift to the first floor only operates if the pressing of the button in the lift is confirmed by the television controller on the floor above. You will see.'

He jabbed at the button, and immediately brilliant television floodlighting flashed on behind armoured glass in the ceiling above. A short pause, then the door to the lift rumbled back. As they got in, the lighting went out again. One floor up, the lift stopped, and they moved out into a big room in semi-darkness On the wall opposite were four panels each ten feet in diameter, dimly lit and with bright numbered dots scattered irregularly across them like a flying control display. In front of each panel stood an electronic control console with two men seated at it. One or two glanced behind as the lift door opened, then they shuffled respectfully when they saw who the visitors were.

'You may remember from your last visit when we were installing them,' said Ulicke, 'that each panel covers one segment of the sanatorium and grounds. The black segment on each shows where the boundary comes of the controlled area, that is to say the perimeter fence. Every device gives out a slightly different signal, which can be decoded electronically by the computer so that a number is projected. Thus every person shows up on here – two hundred non-trusted guards and about three hundred patients can be identified and controlled. The two main gates are covered separately. We have two observers on each screen because we have found that concentration is difficult on so many points of light, and doubling up increases the possibility of noticing unusual behaviour by at least fifty per cent. Herr Kobel, is there anything worth reporting happening at the moment?'

The dark figure at a dimly illuminated desk at right angles to the other eight men, rose and said, 'Yes sir. Number twenty-three appears to be in an unauthorized area.' He pointed to a dot of light that was moving slowly across an otherwise dark section. 'Number ten's light appears to have failed here. It is probably an electrical fault. And number four hundred is running behind schedule on a patrol. You can see his spot of light stationary by the garages there. Unlike the others, he is a guard. All these irregularities are being investigated now.'

'How foolproof is the device, Ulicke?' Stefanopoulos asked.

'Very good indeed now that we have wired all the buildings. There are technical defects, of course. We cannot tell which floor of any particular building a device is on, and the signal becomes too weak to record if, say, an earthed bell of lead is placed over it. But we arrange to paralyse each wearer once early in his time here, and they then develop towards the whole thing a superstitious awe like prim-

147

itive tribes towards their gods. It is, of course, a very upsetting experience.'

He chuckled with pleasure at the success of his invention. 'Perhaps you would like to see the television room?' he said to Stefanopoulos. 'It is down the far end of the same floor. This is a more difficult task. Each observer has ten screens and, of course, he cannot watch them all, particularly if light conditions become unfavourable. But he knows who is a special risk, watches him particularly and logs important data in his record. Also he has each man's daily programme. We have discovered many surprising activities on the part of solitary men who think they are alone. There is at least a chapter for a book on ethnology there.'

'Herr Doktor,' interrupted Kobel, in the calm voice of a man whom nothing surprised any more, 'Number four hundred's light has now gone out as well. He is well clear of the other failure, but I believe it must be deliberate because of his odd behaviour before.'

'Press the paralyser and have him brought in immediately,' snapped Ulicke. 'You have not, I hope, forgotten the affair of a few days ago when that doctor stole the Jaguar? If this man now is near the garages, perhaps he has the same idea. We will go to the television area meanwhile.'

They moved twenty yards along to an open door. This room was also in semi-darkness. Rows of luminously grey television monitors were banked along a wall, and a number of men sat in front of them. Occasionally one would lean forward to adjust the brightness or to turn a frame-hold knob. Each wore a set of earphones, and in his lap was a ten point switch which enabled him to listen in to the patients shown on the set, or to talk through the microphone suspended in front of his face.

'Let me see Fairfax,' said Stefanopoulos. 'That was an arousing demonstration that he gave earlier. It is appropriate that he becomes impotent, otherwise you risk feeling inferior, do you not, Ulicke?'

The heavily built doctor grimaced and answered, 'To be honest, I prefer a good bottle of cognac.' Then he called in German, 'Herr Kruchs, which is the set that shows Mr Rhys, the new patient?'

'This one, Herr Doktor,' said the overseer, walking down the line and pointing it out. The operator concerned turned up the contrast. Fairfax was visible, lying on his bed and reading a book in an attitude of total relaxation.

'Does he do anything unusual?' asked Ulicke.

'We have him under special observation, Herr Doktor,' said the man. 'He is quite sociable and visits other patients – the doctor, Weldon, for example. But his conversations seem harmless.'

'Weldon? He should not visit Weldon. That man knows far too much. These visits are to be stopped immediately.'

'Yes, Herr Doktor.' The operator tuned his switch to Fairfax's wavelength and said evenly, 'Herr Rhys, we forbid you to visit Doctor Weldon in the room next door. Is that clearly understood? You will be paralysed if you go in there again.'

Fairfax waved languidly towards the camera and said loudly, 'OK, sweetheart.'

'The man has arrogance,' said Ulicke crossly. 'That is another of the male characteristics he will lose shortly.'

A buzzer sounded on the overseer's desk. 'It's for you, Herr Doktor,' said the latter holding the handpiece towards Ulicke. 'Herr Kobel reports that number four hundred has disappeared altogether. His device was found smashed on the ground behind the garage.'

Ulicke's face went purple with anger, and he grabbed the telephone to bark, 'I want all available guards immediately in the area by the garage. All cars are to be immobilized immediately and the searchers are to fan out in an organized fashion from that point. The hunt is to continue until the man is found. Who is he, by the way?'

'The guard, Hans Saxo, an ex-skiing instructor. A rather troublesome man.'

'I will come down and direct operations myself,' said Ulicke. He turned to Stefanopolos to say, 'Will you excuse me for a while? I must deal with this crisis personally. The overseer here will escort you back to your quarters.'

'Of course. I would come down with you, but it is not desirable that my face should become known to guards who are not trusties.'

'Naturally,' said Ulicke. 'What would you like to do, Herr Stefanopoulos?'

'It is late to return to Italy in the helicopter. I will sleep here. That girl who tested Fairfax Rhys yesterday impressed me with her energy. Have her sent up to my room, will you?'

'Yes, certainly sir.'

Ulicke barked an order to Kobel over the telephone, then hurried into the lift and was gone, leaving Stefanopoulos to be accompanied back through the sanatorium by the overseer, who set about his task with grovelling respect.

Chapter 17

'For God's sake hurry,' said Sally, standing anxiously by the garage window. 'Hans says that we've only got two minutes before he's recorded overdue'. Puffing with exertion, Myra lifted a lead-acid battery with a bump on to the windowsill. Sally seized it by the handles and struggled across the grass with its weight held low between her legs, while Myra fell out of the window again holding a starter solenoid and two lengths of wire. She ran up to where Hans and Sally stood.

'We will have to be very quick and quiet,' said Hans urgently. 'There are people about in the woods on either side – probably other men going back to the guard block. Now, if this thing goes off and paralyses me, run for your lives. I won't scream for help until I am forced to, and you must be out of the way by then. Now, first of all, I'll take the plunger out of the solenoid. If you will twist one end of each wire firmly round a battery contact, then attach the positive to this screw pin here, and hold the negative against the casing as an earth, it should become a powerful magnet.'

They did as he said. As a test he took a small penknife out of his pocket and stuck the blade into the mouth of the solenoid. With a loud click it was jerked out of sight. Disconnecting the wire quickly from the battery he let the knife drop out again.

'Now comes the dangerous part,' he said, grimacing as he whipped off his black jacket and revealed a powerful brown arm, with the stainless-steel expanding bracelet housed snugly above the biceps. 'If you' – he pointed at Sally – 'will just put the solenoid firmly against the cover and then you' – he pointed at Myra – 'put on the electricity, I'll try to slip a coin under the needle while the spring is held back by the magnet.' Sally and Myra did as they were told. Hans, hands resolutely steady, but a sweat of tension beading on his forehead, said, 'Jesus, I hate these things', through gritted teeth as he slid a two-franc coin up so that its knurled edge rested against the device. 'OK?' he asked tensely.

'As OK as I can make it,' said Sally.

Swiftly he thrust the coin underneath the steel circle. There was no click from inside it. Hans shut his eyes with disbelieving gratitude. For a second he stood still, then voices sounded through the trees to his right. 'Quick,' he said, slipping the bracelet down his arm, the two franc piece held against the underside of it. As it left contact with the solenoid, there was a thud as the injection needle imbedded itself in the soft metal of the coin. In a second he had flung the bracelet to the ground and stamped on it with his heel. Then he grabbed the battery and solenoid and said, 'Quick, we'll hide these and ourselves in the garage.'

Myra scrambled in through the window, followed by the other two. She took the battery and put it and the solenoid back in the rack that she had fetched them from, while Hans carefully shut the window behind them. Then they dodged in between the dark row of cars to the furthest corner.

'There's a door here. Do you know where it leads, Hans?' whispered Sally.

'I think it goes up to the main medical block. We guards are not allowed to use it.' He turned the handle and, somewhat to his surprise, it opened. It was as black as pitch. 'I'll just flick the lights on so that we can see where it runs and whether it's straight. Then I'll turn them off again so that no one knows we've been here.'

A line of bulbs lit up as he pressed the switch, disappearing into the distance several hundred yards away. Except for a ventilation grating in the roof about every twenty yards, the tunnel was quite featureless, and there was no cover in it.

'Perhaps we'd do better in the garage itself?' said Myra.

'Stay by the switch a second,' he said. 'I'll see if we can get up into those shafts.' He ran down to the first dark space, boots echoing thunderously on the concrete. Putting his machine-gun down and reaching up, he forced in the frame of the wire grid. To his surprise, it gave readily on hinges at one side. He reached inside, holding on to the edge of the frame and pulled himself up. There was a surprisingly large circular shaft above, four feet in diameter.

'One of you come here and I'll lift you in. Has either of you got a cigarette lighter?'

Sally said she had, and he asked her to turn out the lights, then to come to the shaft using the lighter, and he would pull her up into it as well. First he lifted Myra and the gun up into the space, and she stood carefully on the concrete lip off the edge of the grating. Echoing darkness shut in as Sally turned out the lights, then found her way up to the shaft by the glimmer of her guttering butane lighter. Bracing his feet on either side of the shaft, Hans bent and fastened his big hands round her wrists, encouraging her to hold him in the same way. Then, with a swift heave, he lifted her up beside them. Gingerly she felt for a foot space, while he shut the grating behind her with his feet.

'It's rather like the London Underground in the rush-hour,' said Myra. 'If anyone touches me up I'll have them for indecent assault.' As she spoke, she leaned luxuriously against Hans' powerful frame.

'We must be very quiet,' he whispered back faintly, 'the sound will carry both up the shaft and down into the tunnel. If anyone comes, stand absolutely still and keep your faces to the wall so that nothing white shows.' The two girls shuffled round. Hans linked arms with them for stability on the narrow ledge, and they waited.

A few minutes passed, then they heard shouts and the muffled sounds of running boots above their heads.

'Those will be guards from Control, sent to look for me,' Hans whispered almost imperceptibly.

The door into the garage crashed open, and boots clattered thunderously beyond the tunnel door. 'Search the garage,' shouted a voice in German. 'I want every car examined, inside the boot, underneath, everywhere.'

Car doors began to open and slam, and bonnet catches clicked open. Above them there were more shouts as men arrived and were instructed to fan out through the woods. Somewhere in the distance an alarm klaxon began to sound.

'It seems to be getting colder,' muttered Sally, 'or is it just the draught up the tunnel?'

'Some snow is forecast for tonight,' answered Hans. 'Occasionally we get snow in June up here.'

'How British you are,' said Myra, 'talking about the bloody weather at a time like this.'

They were silent again. The minutes passed slowly as the sounds of search continued in the garage. Then the door at the end of the tunnel crashed open and a thick, angry voice bellowed, 'Have you looked in there?'

'*Nein, Herr Doktor*,' came the nervous reply.

'Then do so now,' the other thundered.

Steps came nearer. It sounded like two men. Sally, glancing down, could see a few specks of debris that they had dislodged when climbing in, and which now lay directly below them in tell-tale fashion. She shrank into the rough concrete. The steps came nearer, and stopped under the ventilator. Sally felt Hans' muscular body tense alongside her. Out of the corner of her eye, she caught a momentary glimpse of a white face staring up. Whoever it was, mercifully, didn't seem to have a torch. After a moment of straining his eyes into the blank darkness he and his companion moved to the next shaft. Then their steps receded slowly up the tunnel. The faint glimmer of daylight through the louvres at ground level above them had now ceased. It must be nearly dark outside. Cramped and increasingly cold in the dank atmosphere, they stood on, now and then shifting their weight from one foot to another. After twenty minutes the men came back down the tunnel. The door into the garage shut behind them, but the lights stayed on below. The three of them moved closer together for warmth.

'What happens if we're trapped in here for the night?' asked Myra.

'Later, it should be safe for me to walk through to the Medical Block,' said Hans. 'They will not expect me to go there. And perhaps I can find your friend. But I would be happier if they had turned out the light below. If they saw me climbing out of here, then you'd all get caught.'

'Will Fairfax have one of those bracelet things on, do you think?'

'Yes, almost certainly, I'm afraid. We will have to take his off in the same way. And preferably before we take him out of his room at all.'

'I don't understand completely,' said Sally. 'They can track you somehow while you're wearing one of those murderous armband things, but how do they tell if you're in a particular room – surely the apparatus isn't as exact as that?'

'Inside the buildings there are microphones and television cameras in nearly every room used by the patients. They switch between that system and the overhead wire one in the Control Block. It makes it very difficult to deceive them.'

'Is there any way that we can immobilize the Control Block?'

'I can't think of any. The place is designed to withstand shellfire, bombs, anything.'

'Tell me,' said Sally, a thoughtful look on her face in the darkness, 'how does the sanatorium get its electricity supply?'

Hans thought for a moment, then said, 'There's an overhead cable coming up from the valley on pylons. I think that must be it. But we have our own diesel emergency supply up here too. It can be switched on in a matter of minutes if necessary.'

'Do you think you could do something really dangerous for us in return for our freeing you?' Sally went on.

'Of course. A skiing instructor is reared on danger. What do you want?'

'When things have died down a bit outside, could you possibly get out somehow and shoot up the power supply line? It might give us a few minutes' both of darkness and freedom from all these television cameras and things. If you could have a go at the emergency generator as well—' Sally stopped. The tunnel door had opened again, and heavy, deliberate steps were crunching towards them. Sally shrank closer against the others as whoever it was got nearer.

Chapter 18

Fairfax stared out of the window at the unseasonable snowflakes that were falling. Typically unpredictable high Alpine weather. Although he was tired, he did not feel like sleep. He felt instinctively that sinister things were going on, and was half afraid to go to bed in case he missed something. Earlier, he had been forbidden to visit Weldon, the only kindred spirit of any sort that he had met in three days. Then some kind of panic had taken place among the guards. He had watched hundreds of them streaming across the grass from the barrack block in the half light, carrying their guns and disappearing down the slope to the left. The loudspeakers had come on, warning every patient to stay in his room until further notice. Now it was nearly eleven o'clock, and there was still no sign of the guards coming back under the arc-lights which had been switched on all along the frontage of the buildings. He felt helpless, desperately anxious for the girl to come back with the key she had promised him. What could have detained her? She had had an hour and a half. Perhaps she had been caught trying to take a key. Or perhaps the feverish activity of the guards had interfered in some way.

He paced the room. His self-discipline was beginning to fray after three days. With little else to do but observe himself, he had begun to wonder with increasing frequency, what effect the hormone would have on him. His courage might go. His judgement – perhaps he would find that he could only park his car peering round him like an elderly, impotent tortoise. That would mean the end of his livelihood too. What did a bloody castrato do in modern society – get himself hired to guard blamelessly the harem of one of the few surviving grand viziers? He was moving towards the window at the precise moment that he heard the unmistakable rattle of a machine-gun a few hundred yards away. A long burst – it sounded like a whole magazine. And just as it ended, with total suddenness, every light in sight went out. He stood for a moment disbelievingly. If the lights were out, the television cameras could not see. He'd make sure their darkness was permanent. Feeling for the thermostat on the wall, he jabbed viciously at it with a chair leg. Glass from the lens tinkled to the floor.

He wrenched the door open just as the guard at the far end bellowed, 'Everyone must stay in his room. I will shoot anyone who comes out.' Still holding his chair, Fairfax crept down the corridor towards the other man. His rubber-soled shoes made no sound but the faintest scuffle as he walked, but the other man heard him. A loud click sounded as the other cocked the action of his automatic.

'Stop there, whoever you are, or I shoot,' the guard screamed in German. Fairfax halted for a nerve-tingling second, hair rising on the back of his neck in the oppressive silence. Then he hurled the chair with all his strength down the corridor, at the same moment throwing himself flat in the angle at the base of the corridor wall. The chair grazed the wall as it hurtled along, and simultaneously the guard fired at the sound. He was still shooting when it hit him, legs first, and he cried out with fear and pain. His bullets had whined down the corridor at crazy ricocheting angles, but Fairfax was unscathed.

He gave the guard no time to recover, but rose in a crouch and leapt towards him, windmilling his arms. The man fired once more before Fairfax reached him in the darkness, but his shot went so wide that it thudded into the ceiling somewhere behind. Then Fairfax's right hand crunched on flesh and bone. There was no doubt about it:

the man must be killed. Identifying the big man's solar plexus in the darkness, Fairfax smashed his elbow into it with a karate blow, feeling something give sickeningly at the same moment as the other gave a harsh cry that was no longer human. The revolver banged again, but this time in a senseless reflex and the bullet slammed harmlessly into the wall. The man crumpled, and Fairfax felt for the guard's windpipe and crashed his hand edge down on to it as he lay on the ground. Silence. Bruised and trembling with tension, Fairfax bent to feel round for the revolver. He found it still clutched in the guard's right hand, so tightly that he put on the safety catch before trying to free it, in case the dead man's fingers pulled the trigger. There was no sound from any of the patients' rooms, and he imagined them cowering like old women inside. Feeling his way along the wall, he counted ten doors to Weldon's, then went in.

'Hello there, Taffy. I've just done the guard in the darkness out there,' he said.

'By Golly, I thought it was the bloody Cardiff Town Rugby Team having a beer up,' said the other delightedly.

'I was proposing to beat it out of here. Are you prepared to come along?' said Fairfax.

'Nice of you to ask me, but I think I'd hold you up too much in my bloody condition.'

'Don't be ridiculous. I'll carry you. We probably haven't got more than a few minutes. How do you feel?'

'Marvellous at the mere thought of getting out.' The weights on his leg crashed to the floor as he undid them, and his bed creaked loudly as he wriggled to the edge of it.

Fairfax turned to lift him carefully on to his back, saying, 'Thank God you know your way round this place a bit. How do we get down to the ground floor now the lift's out of action?' He stood up, Weldon on his back.

The other grunted with pain from his smashed leg, then said,

'There's a fire escape, the last door on the right. It goes down to the hall.'

Staggering slightly in the complete darkness, Fairfax felt his way back down the passage, walking carefully the last few yards, to avoid the body of the guard. He turned into the staircase door, and felt with his feet for the edge of the top stair. Despite the pain any fall would cause him, Weldon said nothing as he felt Fairfax groping his way down uncertainly. At last they reached the bottom and pushed open the door into the hall.

'Make for the garage tunnel,' said Weldon, 'we can probably bust the door down somehow.'

'I've got the guard's gun,' said Fairfax, 'I'll have a go at shooting the lock off. Can I safely put you down?'

'Don't worry about me,' said Weldon. 'I can just about stand on one leg while you get on with it.'

Gently, Fairfax lowered Weldon, conscious that at any moment the lights might come on again. He patted round the wall near where Weldon had said the door was. After what seemed hours, he found the slightly recessed square frame and the metal plaque of a Yale-type lock. He drew the gun, pushed off the safety catch and said, 'I hope that you're not frightened of bangs.'

There was a deafening explosion, and Fairfax felt splinters of wood and metal hail against his knuckles where he held the gun. He pushed the door and it gave. 'Come on, my friend,' he said picking him up and heading for the steep flight of steps into the tunnel. Weldon's stiffly plastered leg kept catching on the rough wall on the way down.

'Sorry, boyo,' he said. 'There's nothing I can do about it. If you want to try and stagger down without me then—' At that moment it caught unexpectedly on something, and Weldon could not stop himself crying out sharply with the pain.

'Jesus, what's that – is there someone there?' said Fairfax, feeling inexplicably another human presence in the immediate vicinity. He couldn't get at his gun without dropping Weldon, and that was unthinkable.

'Fairfax!' shrieked a woman's voice a few inches away in the darkness. 'Fairfax, darling! How marvellous.'

'Sally—?' he said disbelieving. 'What in hell's name are you doing here?'

'Oh, how tremendous, you're safe, everything's going to be all right,' said Sally, tears suddenly in her voice. In the darkness she flung her arms indiscriminately round the two men.

'Hallo, ducky,' said Weldon. 'Nice to meet you, whoever you are.'

'Sally, this is Doctor Peter Weldon – you remember the man who crashed the Jaguar?'

'But he was dead. You said so.'

'He was. But that was just one of his nine lives, I'm glad to say.'

Thankfully, Fairfax had reached the level floor of the tunnel. He stopped for a moment to rest. Just as he lowered Weldon's feet gently to the floor, the tunnel lights came on brilliantly white.

'God Almighty,' said Sally. 'Hans and Myra went off to cut the electricity wires – someone must either have mended them, or they've got the emergency supply going.'

'It's going to be very dangerous going down the tunnel in the light, but we've got no option really. Who's Hans, anyway?' asked Fairfax.

'He's a guard that we persuaded to join us.' Blinking in the light, Sally stared at Fairfax, then said, 'You've lost pounds of weight and look terrible, but at least you're alive.' Again she flung her arms round his neck and kissed him.

'I hate to remind you at this moment of romantic reunion,' said Weldon, 'but you have got one of those paralyser things on your arm. As far as I know this tunnel is not wired, but you can't bank on it, and Ulicke is just the kind of man to knock off everyone in a panic and worry about the antidote afterwards.'

'We've found a way of getting those things off safely,' said Sally. 'We did it on Hans earlier this evening. If we can just get down to the garage at the far end, I'm sure I can do the same for you.'

'All right, let's try,' said Fairfax. 'I'll carry Peter because he can't walk. Here, take the gun, Sally. It's only got a couple of rounds left in it, but they'll be quite useful in a passage as narrow as this.'

She took the gun and walked quickly towards the garage. Fairfax picked up his friend, wincing a little at the way the other's weight dragged at the healing wound in his shoulder. Even walking as quietly as they could, the sound of their footsteps sounded off a loud echo. They were about halfway down when, as abruptly as they had come on, the lights went out again.

Fairfax stopped and called quietly to Sally, 'Hang on a moment. Myra and Hans may have got at the generator. Alternatively, there may be someone on the light switch at the end of the tunnel.'

They stood for a moment in silence. Then, through the ventilators above the ground came angry shouts and a long burst of automatic fire.

'OK, let's go on,' said Fairfax. 'That sounds as if there are plenty of distractions upstairs.' He moved on slowly, conscious that hitting Weldon's injured leg inadvertently against the wall caused the latter exquisite pain. At last they reached the garage door.

Sally put her mouth to Fairfax's ear and kissed him momentarily before saying, 'There may be a guard, in the garage. Do you mind going in first while I look after Peter? If all's clear, I'll come and get the bits to get that device off your arm.'

'Of course, my angel,' he answered, taking the gun from her and tiptoeing through into the big, petrol-smelling space of the garage beyond. It was as silent as a mausoleum, and nearly as dark. He collided with the black hull of a car, and muttered a curse. There might be other hazards – a sunken pit or a ramp, for instance. His cautiously moving foot touched an empty oil can. Picking it up, he hurled it into the darkness. It hissed away for twenty yards, then clattered against the wall and rolled to a standstill. In the garage there was no other sound, although outside there were still yells in the distance and occasional shots.

Concluding that there was no one inside the garage waiting for him to make a target of himself, he reached into the nearest car and turned on the sidelights. Their restrained glow, reflecting from the light concrete ceiling, gave enough light for Fairfax to see the row of cars stretching away down to the far end. He turned back to the tunnel.

'There's no one about,' he said to the others, 'but I wouldn't exclude the possibility of someone coming back at any moment. Can you do your stuff straight away, Sally, please?'

'Of course,' the girl answered. She went to the shelf of stores by the window and took down the battery and overdrive solenoid that they had used before. Fairfax, with the dreadful recollection of the last time he had tried to interfere with the device, felt his mouth going dry with fear as he rolled up the sleeve of his denim blouse. Sally connected up the solenoid matter-of-factly, and tested that it was working by pulling the plunger out a couple of times and letting it snap back.

'Hans used a two-franc piece, to put under the needle while we held the spring back with the magnet,' said Sally. 'Have you got anything like that on you?'

'Not a cent,' said Fairfax.

'Nor me,' said Weldon, propped uncomfortably against the wing of a Porsche.

'Oh well, I'd better have a look round for something,' said Sally. She rummaged about on the shelves in the dim light, finally coming back to them with a flat spanner of blued metal. 'I'm afraid this is the best I can find. Now, I'll put the magnet over the thing, like this—'
So saying, she connected the wires from the device to one pole of the

battery, holding the silvery casing of the solenoid hard against the other. Fairfax tried not to show his fear and, despite the cold, felt sweat accumulating above his thick eyebrows.

'Now,' said Sally, 'without pushing my magnet away, work the handle end of the spanner under the edge.' Fairfax hesitated.

'Go on, darling,' she said encouragingly. 'I promise it won't go off.' With sudden resolution, he thrust the metal end under, waiting an anguished moment for the click. None came.

'Right,' she said. 'Now I'll take off the solenoid and the needle will just go into the metal spanner.' A few drops of liquid ran coldly down Fairfax's arm as the needle shot out and broke off against the spanner.

'Right, I'll take the damn thing off,' he said, wrenching the bracelet down his arm, 'then we'll try starting a car and see how far we can get.'

'I promised that I'd wait here for Myra until two a.m.,' said Sally. 'What time is it now?'

'Half past one. We'll have to find somewhere to hide for half an hour. Perhaps in one of the cars? I'd like to choose one and make briefly sure the engine'll run.' He walked away down the parked line. Mostly they were Mercedes, with half-a-dozen armoured cars bristling with machine-guns down the far end and, in between, a few Porsches, Jaguars and humble Volkswagens. He chose a 500 SE and walked back to carry Weldon down and deposit him on the back seat.

Chapter 19

Myra shivered, wishing that she had brought another sweater. She and Hans were standing directly under the power line that came up from the valley, waiting for sounds of the search to die down in the neighbourhood. At last they could hear no one nearer than 100 yards away.

'It should be OK now,' Myra whispered.

'Here goes then,' said Hans. He snapped back the action of his machine pistol and pointed it up at the insulators outlined against the dim blue clouds of the night sky. For a moment he peered to find the luminous foresight. Then there came an ear-splitting blast of sound as he pulled the trigger. Flames from the muzzle streaked into the sky, and blue-white sparks danced and crackled as the bullets smashed the ceramic insulators and tore at the thick wire. The gun thundered on, until the firing pin clicked on an empty magazine.

Myra, her back to the pyrotechnic display at the top of the pole, said matter-of-factly, 'You've done it. All the sanatorium lights have gone out.'

'Come on, we must run for it. They'll be round here in seconds.' Taking her arm, he dragged her back up towards the dark mass of the clinical building.

As they ran, a long burst of fire came from somewhere to their right, but it was obviously not aimed at them because no bullets hissed past. Hans had said that he would lead her at once to the emergency generator, nervous as he was that the enemy would immediately put a guard on it, expecting further sabotage. They panted up the path while all round them orders were shouted and men crashed through the thin undergrowth. At the top of the slope the path emerged from the trees, and Hans and Myra slowed to a walk to attract less attention if they should pass anyone in the dark.

The generator was in a low concrete building, separated by a few yards from the main structure to keep the noise of the big diesel from disturbing those inside. As they got nearer, they saw a small group of figures round the open door, and inside a wavering light.

Hans stopped, then whispered, 'With my uniform, they will not realize that I am against them until it is too late. But you must stay here. I will come back for you in a minute.'

Myra stood still, feeling lonely and exposed in the middle of the large area of grass. Hans moved quietly on. The group by the door did not seem to hear him until he was right on top of them, then she heard him say, 'Hands up,' in German, pointing his reloaded machine pistol at the three men who stood there, their weapons slung over their shoulders.

They did as they were ordered, mingled fear and surprise showing on their faces in the dim reflected light from the torch inside. Hans glanced in and saw two men still bent unsuspectingly over the control panel of the emergency generator. He called, 'Myra', over his shoulder and she ran to where he stood.

'Please take a gun from one of these men and keep them covered while I go inside. And watch for reinforcements coming up from elsewhere.' She took one of the heavy little guns, cocked it and snapped the safety catch off.

'Put your guns down one at a time on the ground beside me,' she ordered in French, watching with concealed anxiety in case one of the two men who were still armed went rogue in the dim light. The first man put his gun down. The second was just about to, when the torchlight suddenly went out. The blackness was almost complete. She heard Hans shout from inside the building and, at the same moment put her foot on the gun on the ground. For a moment, the man who was still armed did nothing. Myra, a great believer in striking first, said loudly, 'If either of you moves a muscle, I will shoot you both.'

Immediately she had spoken, a shot reverberated inside the generating room, followed by a crash, then a burst from Hans' machine pistol, followed by a heavy silence.

'Put your gun down now,' she demanded, going so close to the dark shape of the man who was still armed to be able to prod him in the ribs with the muzzle of her gun. Obviously alarmed by the trigger happiness of her companion, he let his weapon fall with a thud to the grass.

Another solitary shot came from inside, followed by an answering burst from Hans. Kicking the second spare gun out of the way, Myra sidled into the doorway. She assumed that the two men who had been working on the generator had now taken cover behind the metal hull of the big machine, in which case they would be rather difficult to dislodge, but at least they would not be able to start the thing from there.

This thought had just gone through her head when she heard the starter motor begin to whirr and the diesel engine chuffing with ever increasing speed. Hans' gun blazed again, but the dynamo hummed implacably faster, a relay crashed over, and the lights came on brilliantly in the block nearby, lighting up the faces of the three men near her so clearly that Myra could even see the colour of their eyes as they blinked at her. There was still no light in the engine room and, realizing that she was now silhouetted against the bright windows behind her, Myra hurriedly moved out of the doorway and against

167

the rough wall. What should she do now? If she went inside and left her three prisoners, they would run off to give the alarm. If she didn't help Hans, he might be detained for some time and meanwhile, with the camp lights on, Sally would not be able to try and rescue Fairfax.

There was a long silence in the darkness inside, with occasional faint, deadly scuffling sounds. She imagined Hans crawling through the machinery, and the others waiting eagerly for him to get close enough to shoot. The silence dragged on and on. Her prisoners watched her in silent unease, and behind them she saw a tall man in black uniform coming towards them from about seventy metres away. Just then, a naked bulb inside the powerhouse came on blindingly. Instantaneously, Hans' machine pistol stuttered and a man screamed. She glanced in. Hans stood with his back against the doorpost by the light switch, smoking gun directed at where the technicians had been hidden. There was no sign of anyone else. Snapping on another magazine, he took aim at the big switchboard and the gun battered away while glass tinkled from shattered dials.

As the bullets chewed away the main fuses there was an explosive short-circuit and darkness descended again. The lights gave Myra a last glimpse of the big man breaking into a run over the grass, hauling his pistol out of his holster as he came. Taking a resolute grip of the oily barrel in her fingers, Myra jerked the trigger and hosed a burst into the sudden blackness. Hans appeared behind her.

'Get in, you bastards,' he shouted to the prisoners, thrusting them roughly down the steps into the powerhouse and slamming and locking the heavy metal door.

'Mind out,' said Myra, 'there's an armed man out there somewhere. Come this way.' She dragged him by the arm at right angles to the direction from which she had seen the advancing man. To her surprise, no shots came as they ran. Myra became aware that something was getting into her eyes. After a moment she realized that it was fine flakes of snow, getting steadily harder. That would make life difficult if they couldn't get out of the camp now, because they would leave tracks everywhere, like hunted animals.

Hans slowed his loping gait. 'Careful, someone's coming. Let's stop here,' he said, pulling her into the shelter of a hut where the machines that mowed the grass were stored. A group of about a dozen men marched past, flashing torches round them in a nervous fashion and holding their guns at the ready.

He grinned as they moved out of earshot and whispered to her, 'You see how it is when a modern civilization gets used to all its gadgets? People go completely to pieces when the gadgets fail.'

'You're a mad bugger,' said Myra. 'How did they manage to keep you a prisoner all this time?'

He shrugged. 'You can get used to anything in this life,' he said. 'They were not too bad; the only thing was that I was not free, and at my age you cannot forgive loss of your freedom.'

'Do you know where Stefanopoulos is?' asked Myra. 'As a last gesture before we go, I'd like to shoot him.'

'Who is he then?' asked the other puzzledly.

'The ultimate boss of the place, I think,' said the girl. 'I was his mistress for five years, but the thought revolts me now that I know what he was up to all the time.'

'Ah, the big boss. Yes, an enormous man. He came yesterday in a helicopter. I did not know his name. He will be sleeping in Ulicke's flat upstairs. We can find him if you want.'

Myra thought for a moment, then said, 'No, I couldn't bring myself to do him in, no matter what he's done. I just hope he chokes, that's all. Let's get back to the garage.' She linked her arm with his, and they moved off.

Chapter 20

'**H**ow are Myra and Hans going to get in? Is the window still open?' asked Sally. She was comfortably entwined on the front passenger seat of the Mercedes with Fairfax, while Weldon lay down out of sight in the back.

'I've no idea,' said Fairfax. 'Aren't the main doors unlocked?'

'They weren't earlier.'

'Well, I'd better go and fix the window open. Keep out of sight everyone, just in case I have any problems.'

Quietly he undid the car door and slipped out, gripping the pistol in his right hand as he felt his way down the line of cars to the end wall. The window was closed but with the catch undone. Holding the handle firmly, he edged the metal frame open. Something made him stop for a few seconds when there was a gap of only two inches. From just along the wall there came a slight grating sound. He strained his eyes into the darkness. A dim shape slowly came into focus no more than six feet away. As Fairfax tried to see if the other was alone, some small particles fell into his eyes. At first he thought it was dust, then he remembered that it would be snow.

There was obviously a guard on the garage. And if Hans and Myra were not extremely careful, they would get caught and probably shot as they tried to get in. Leaving the window, he walked to the first garage door and found, as he half expected, a small subsidiary door in the main one.

It was padlocked. Fetching a thick screwdriver from the bench nearby, he edged it under the metal clasp as far as his strength would take it, then wrenched it up. The sound of the screws splintering out of the wood echoed deafeningly in the hollow silence of the garage. Without waiting to see if the guard's attention had been attracted, Fairfax darted outside and along the front of the building in the opposite direction from the guard.

It was snowing hard enough now to be a slippery on the concrete apron. The extra care which this made necessary was more than justified when he rounded the corner at the end because another guard stood by the corresponding window there. This one was smoking, his cigarette glowing brightly in the dark. Doubling back, then circling out a fifty yard arc into the darkness, Fairfax mounted the earth-covered back of the garage where it moulded almost imperceptibly into the hillside. Treading carefully to avoid tripping in case there were any obstructions, he approached the edge above the first guard's head, trying to judge it so that he first appeared directly above him. It was now snowing even harder. He had turned up the collar of his thin denims, but the cold bit through progressively as the flakes melted in his body warmth. From up on top he had a view of quite an area of the lower grounds of the sanatorium. There were less signs of confusion among the guards now. The lights of organized groups were visible through the trees, and there was no shouting.

Dropping to his knees to be more stable, he bent over the edge. The black ski cap of the guard was silhouetted against the light snowfall and within touching distance below him. Putting on the heavy pistol's safety catch, Fairfax leaned over and crunched the barrel against the man's temple. Without a sound, the guard crumpled forward on to the snowy grass. Fairfax dropped the eight feet down to where the other lay to take his sub-machine-gun and the handful of magazines from the webbing bag on his belt.

As the guard was clearly only stunned, Fairfax knew he would recover quickly. After hesitating for a moment, he took off the man's black skijacket and put it on himself. If he was going to stay outside until Hans and Myra came, it would be impossible without this extra warmth. But first he must deal with the other guard so that when the time came they could force the doors and drive away without being shot at.

Again he padded over the roof, repeating his careful approach to the over-hanging edge. But this time, to his surprise, he could no longer see anyone below. He wasted a further couple of minutes searching the apron from above but there was no sign of anyone there either. For some obscure reason, the guard had obviously gone. Returning to the first window and crouching against the flurries of snow, he began to run over in his mind what still remained to be done. He had not dared to start the engine of the Mercedes earlier in case the noise attracted someone, but a quick check had shown that although the keys were in the ignition, fuses had been removed from the box to make the car difficult to start. Whoever had removed them it had not been very intelligent because, by the flame of Sally's lighter, Fairfax had found without difficulty a box of replacement fuses in the stores. There was petrol in the tank and juice in the battery. It should go at first touch.

A slight noise came out of the silently flurrying snow ahead. He only knew from Sally that Hans was a big man and dressed as a guard. If he came along it would be a risky moment while he decided whether it was him or just another one of the enemy. A shadow moved in front of him. He slipped off the safety catch and pointed the gun at it. Then he saw unmistakably that it was a woman.

'Myra,' he called softly, 'it's Fairfax here.'

The girl stopped briefly then came on, saying, 'You marvellous man-mountain. We were told you'd been turned into a woman.'

'I believe I have, but it doesn't show yet – I hope,' he answered. 'Congratulations on your job on the lights. Where's Hans?'

'He's following me at a decent distance. Be along in just a second. Have you got a car going? Where's Sally?'

'She's in the Mercedes we picked. And we've got a badly injured British doctor as well. He was the chap I saw crash that Jaguar on the Gotthard.'

'Good Heavens, I thought he was dead.'

'So did everybody else. But he's not.'

Another shadow materialized. Myra, afraid lest Hans should mistake Fairfax in his black anorak for an intruding guard, called huskily to him, 'Hans, come on, it's all right.' She introduced the two men briefly.

'We'd better hurry now,' said Fairfax, 'there's an unconscious guard here liable to wake any minute, and another one at the far end who's disappeared in mysterious circumstances.'

He helped Myra through the window he had left open. Hans followed him, then Fairfax. The latter was barely inside when he realized that something was wrong. He heard boots grating on the concrete, then, almost instantly, a powerful torch caught them. They had slung their arms in order to get through the window, and none of them could do anything instantly when the voice behind the light screamed in German, 'Put your pistols down immediately or I shoot!' Hans dropped his sub-machine-gun followed by Fairfax.

'*Jetzt, alle Hände hoch*' yelled the man. 'Who are you? You are the prisoner Rhys, aren't you?' He flashed the torch beam jerkily at Fairfax. None of the three said anything, anxious to spin out the moment so as to gain a little time. 'Answer me,' he thundered. 'Who are you?' He moved nearer, his boots rasping harshly.

'My name's Myra Howe, if you must know, you impudent peasant,' said the girl in a haughty upper-class accent, 'and which Borstal have you escaped from?'

174

The other was obviously nonplussed. '*Was sagen Sie?*' he said uncertainly. As he spoke, there was a soggy thud and the torch and whoever held it crashed to the floor.

'It's all right, there was just the one lout in here,' said Sally cheerfully, coming up to them. 'Peter and I heard him come through the door that you forced, Fairfax. He was prowling about for some time. I never realized before how difficult it is to open a car door silently.'

'What did you hit him with, my sweetest,' asked Myra, 'your handbag?'

'No, I am afraid it was a jack handle – the only thing I could find. He's going to have a dreadful headache when he wakes up.'

'Come on everybody,' said Fairfax, 'we must get out of here now. Sally and Myra to the car please. Sally, start the engine while Hans and I force the doors.'

The two men picked up their guns and the guard's rubber torch, and went to the big doors. To Fairfax's surprise, the old trick of pulling out the floor bolt on one side enabled them to disengage the mortise lock in the middle with a powerful push and the doors swung open. Behind them, the Mercedes engine had started, and Sally was gunning the big V8 to a couple of thousand revs to warm it. Fairfax swiftly changed places with her, handing his weapon to Weldon in the back, who said, 'I can't bloody well stand up, but sitting down with this I'll be a match for anyone.'

Thrusting the lever into first gear and switching on the full headlight beams, Fairfax sent the big car surging out on to the concrete apron.

Chapter 21

Stefanopoulos, his shoes off, waited on the large and comfortable bed in Ulicke's guest suite. He was not accustomed to being kept waiting by anyone. The overseer had said that he would bring the Italian girl immediately, and that was twenty minutes ago. His dark eyes had a dangerous gleam in them as he drew impatiently on a small cigar.

Ulicke had done a good job scientifically, but there were things about his organization which could definitely be bettered. The escape of the British doctor, for instance, and those madmen who had invaded his island in their plane. Perhaps the solution was to give the disciplinary part of the responsibilities to someone better qualified, leaving Ulicke just to fiddle about with his hormones and armbands.

Someone knocked on the door. It was the overseer. 'Please forgive me for the delay, sir,' said the man, rubbing his hands together ingratiatingly with a scaly sound. 'The girl was difficult to find, and many of the staff are out searching the grounds.' Behind him, scowling resentfully, stood the Italian girl.

'Come here, my darling,' said Stefanopoulos, beckoning to her. She came slowly and uncertainly towards him. Stefanopoulos patted the bed beside him and invited, 'Sit down.'

The girl did so, her lips curling. Stefanopoulos was resentful of any lack of enthusiasm for him; he met it so rarely from the film starlets that he had come to think of himself as irresistible.

Muttering apologies, the German overseer was just about to go when the lights suddenly went out.

'What in the name of Jesus has happened now?' barked Stefanopoulos, thoughts of seduction suddenly vanishing from his mind.

The overseer came back into the room to wheedle, 'I am afraid, sir, that the power supply has failed. But do not be afraid, in seconds the emergency supply will be running.'

'All right. I'll make you personally responsible for ensuring that the breakdown is attended to immediately.'

'Of course, of course.'

The door shut. Stefanopoulos felt out in the darkness for one of the girl's breasts and fastened his fingers on its resilient peak. 'Why do women always pretend that they don't like making love as much as men?' he asked conversationally. 'Basically you are all whores, just as we all are satyrs.'

He didn't finish. The girl whipped a stinging slap at him, which, in the darkness, hit him on the bridge of the nose and made him see stars. 'By the Virgin, I'll rape you for that,' he shouted with unconscious humour.

But the girl was gone, running for her life to the door and beyond. She had promised Fairfax a key and already she felt that she had let him down. In the years at the sanatorium she had fulfilled her duties of nurse and professional exciter, but now something had snapped and all she wanted to do was to get away and into normality.

Still shoeless, Stefanopoulos groped a few yards down the passage, then decided that the girl knew the geography a lot better than he and he would have to let her go. Back in his room, he found his shoes and pulled them on, then felt round for the internal phone, but the receiver was dead. The system must get its power from the mains as well. Cursing out loud, Stefanopoulos made for the door, flashing his lighter to avoid colliding with the furniture. Down the passage he found the fire exit stairs after remembering that the lift would not be working. There seemed to be no one about. The whole building was silent and empty. He came out in the open air. A man in uniform was running past, along the building.

'Here, you,' thundered Stefanopoulos, 'what in the name of fornication is going on here? Has everybody gone mad?'

'There is someone loose with a machine pistol, sir, who has cut the electricity supply. We are working on the emergency generator now.' Stefanopoulos recognized the tall man as one of the doctors.

'Where is the emergency supply?' asked Stefanopoulos.

'About one hundred metres along the wall here, sir,' the man answered. 'I was just going there.'

At that second, the sound of a shot came from the direction in which he pointed, followed by a blast of machine-gun fire which echoed against the cliff-like wall above them.

'Sounds like trouble,' said Stefanopoulos. 'Go and take charge there,' and then added, 'I don't want any blunders. Send Ulicke to me as soon as he can be found. I want to speak to him.'

'I do not know where Herr Ulicke is,' said the man 'but—'

At that moment the lights came on again behind them.

'Thank God for that. Now it should be possible to get some kind of discipline going again,' said Stefanopoulos.

'I'll do my best,' said the doctor.

He ran off into the darkness, unbuttoning his holster. He was still only a few yards away when a rattle of shots came from the low building towards which he was running. The ricochets from the bullets clattered against the concrete and one smashed a window above Stefanopoulos' head. Then the lights went out again.

'Enough is enough,' said Stefanopoulos. 'I'm getting out of here.'

As it had begun to snow, the helicopter was clearly out of the ques-

179

tion. It would have to be a car. He went back into the building, trying to remember from his last visit, months ago, where the tunnel to the garage was. Then, as he walked slowly down the long passage, someone came up behind, running with a wavering torch. It was Ulicke. 'Ach, Herr Stefanopoulos,' he said. 'I am very sorry. Nothing like this has ever happened here before.'

'It's bloody disgraceful,' said the big man coldly. 'Now you are to get me out of here before I get shot. I'd never have come at all if I'd had any idea what a shambles your operation was.'

'Yes, sir. As I say, it has never been like this before. We will take my car. I will drive you back to Italy straightaway. This way please.'

Stefanopoulos stalked along behind as Ulicke obsequiously lit his way with the torch. At last they came to the hallway. Ulicke saw the tunnel door swinging open, and did not notice that the lock had been blasted apart until he tried to shut it behind them. His jowls wobbling with rage, he said, 'Someone has destroyed the lock with a shot. That can only be because they are after the cars. We must hurry, sir.'

'Didn't you order the garage to be guarded, for God's sake?' asked Stefanopoulos.

'Yes, sir, but the guards will probably be on the outside.'

Instinctively ducking under the low ceiling, Stefanopoulos followed the waddling figure ahead of him. As they got nearer to the far end, they heard the sound of an engine throbbing at high revs. 'What's that?' said the doctor, breaking into a run. 'No one has permission to leave the sanatorium.'

Their steps thundered in the confined space. Ulicke wrenched open the door at the far end. As he did so, with a shriek of accelerating tyres, they saw a large black car race for the open doors and vanish into the night with a roar.

'Come on,' shouted Stefanopoulos. 'Which is your car? That was Rhys with a carful of people. After him.'

With surprising speed, Ulicke leapt for his silver Porsche.

'Fortunately the car's not immobilized like the others because it already has an immobilizer,' he said, getting behind the wheel and starting the engine all in the same movement.

'A lot of good immobilizing that Mercedes did,' snapped back Stefanopoulos.

The Porsche plunged out of the garage, headlights flaring on the snowflakes. Despite his bulk and coarse hands, Ulicke was a delicate and courageous driver. Tyres slithering on the patina of snow, he sent the Porsche careering round the bend and out of the yard at a speed most men would have thought suicidal. The lights of the Mercedes had already disappeared.

'The gate will stop him,' said Ulicke, 'it is locked, and very solid.'

'How far is it to the gate?'

'About three kilometres. It's a very winding road. I can take it faster than him.'

'You think so? He's a professional stunt driver.' Stefanopoulos felt behind him for a safety belt and snapped it round his shoulders and waist. On the bends the silvery boles of pine trees loomed up; then, just as it seemed that the car must smash itself into them, Ulicke put it into a slide that felt as if at any moment the heavy rear engine would spin the car completely. Once Ulicke slightly misjudged because of Stefanopoulos's weight and the back thumped the grass bank. The car went on with undiminished speed and neither man spoke.

Already the fresh tracks of the Mercedes shadowed across the snow. Sometimes in the hairpins they became broad swathes where the other car had lost its adhesion and slid sideways.

Loaded with fresh, damp snow, the low branches over the road swayed in the slipstream turbulence from the Mercedes in front. A large white mass detached itself and landed on the windscreen of the Porsche as Ulicke peered through it at the fresh tracks ahead. He shouted, '*Scheisse!*' and whipped on the wipers, slowing momentarily before slamming the accelerator to the floor, to take the next corner sideways.

Chapter 22

'God, what a pig of a night to play tricks on the road in an over-loaded family saloon,' said Fairfax. The big steering wheel was sawing through his hands continuously as he put full reverse lock on to correct the slides each time the car came out of a bend.

'Keep the doors locked and your heads low, everybody,' he said. 'I could always skid off the road and I don't want anybody going out through a door or window.'

'What happens when we get down to the gate?' asked Hans. 'It's almost certainly locked.'

'Can I crash it?'

'No, it's more solid than the car – but wait a minute, I seem to remember there is a manual lever for when the power fails: I'll have to look with a torch when we get down there.'

'You'll have to hurry,' said Fairfax, 'there's a car following us, and it's not losing ground.'

Everyone in the car turned to stare backwards as the Mercedes bucketed crazily through a double bend. Through the snow and trees several hairpins above them, they could see the flash of headlights, and occasionally a gleam of crimson as the other car's brake lights came on.

'He's after us all right. When I stop at the gates, I'll get out with

Peter's gun and shoot the hell out of whoever it is, while Hans tries to work the gates. I should think he's about twenty-five seconds behind, so we won't have long.'

'The gate's round the next bend,' said Hans laconically.

With undiminished speed, Fairfax took the last bend, then wrenched on the handbrake. Crabbing on, the car was still lurching forward at 40 miles an hour when Hans jumped out one side, and Fairfax, grabbing the gun, on the other.

'Keep your heads down in the car out of the shooting,' he said to the others, crouching by the front wing with his gun levelled at the corner round which the following car must come.

There was a crash from the gate as Hans shattered a padlock on the lever with a desperate blow from the gun butt, then threw his full weight on the metal handle. Half frozen, the bolt groaned back. Hans kicked at the heavy metal gates. Lights splashed the snowy bank of the corner 100 metres behind them as the Porsche crabbed round it.

Stefanopoulos had Ulicke's big pistol out of the window. While the car juddered and swerved, he began firing with the cool aim of the expert that he was. His first shot starred the white paint of the gate two inches from Hans' face, just as the latter turned to run back to the car, the gates now being sufficiently open for them to squeeze through. His second shot tore a furrow in the metal of the Mercedes' roof. Then Fairfax fired a long burst at the other car. One headlight went out, and it spun round completely so that the gunman's window was on the blind side. Hans and Fairfax jumped back into the Mercedes. Over-accelerating wheels spinning desperately, the car then leaped for the gap with one side of the gate jarring their flank as it hit just in front of the back wheel.

'Did we fix them for good, Hans?' he asked, fighting the wheel as the car began a long, tearing slide with a drop of hundreds of feet waiting on one side.

184

Hans was screwed round in his seat, and did not answer for a moment. Then, as shafts of light gleamed behind them again, he said, 'No. They're coming on again. The car is being driven by Ulicke. He's got a great reputation as a driver.'

The Porsche came into view again. Ulicke had switched on some dazzling quartz-iodine spotlights to replace the headlamp that Fairfax had blinded. It was impossible to say what other damage had been done. Certainly its speed was undiminished.

'The danger will come at the straights down in the valley,' said Fairfax. 'There he can catch me in a few yards.'

Sweating with concentration and tension, he wrestled with the steering of the heavy car. The Porsche was taking no risks, staying one corner behind them until conditions improved. Fairfax took the Mercedes violently into a bend. As they slid through it, Weldon lost his handhold in the back and toppled, cursing, off the seat. The unexpected movement of his heavy body inside the car caught Fairfax off-guard, and the slide worsened uncontrollably.

'Hold on, everybody,' he shouted as the spinning back tyres mounted the low bank and jerked towards the drop into the woods dozens of feet below. At the last second, there was a bang as a wheel hit a granite rock at the edge and the sideslip stopped. The car had come almost to a halt.

Hans wound his window down and his gun chattered a dozen rounds at the careering car behind. Slipping into second, Fairfax started off again. There was a splintering sound from the rear window, and chips of glass fell on the back seat passengers as a bullet hacked its way through.

They came to the main road. Down here, the snow had turned to rain. Fairfax took the road towards Gletsch, three miles away. This was the moment Ulicke had waited for. In seconds, his incredibly powerful car had caught them, all lights switched out to make it less of a target. Fairfax only saw at the last minute through the starred rear window how close it was, and swerved to block Ulicke's passing manoeuvre.

Ulicke immediately jinked to the other side, then back again. This time he got his bonnet level with the boot of the Mercedes. Tortured metal ground together as Fairfax deliberately side-swiped him. In less capable hands, the Porsche, being the lighter car, would have left the road. But Ulicke somehow held it rock steady, thundering along the wet verge at over eighty miles an hour. The pistol in the other car began banging again.

A side window in the Mercedes shattered into millions of fragments. 'Bugger this,' shouted Weldon, thrusting the muzzle of his gun through into the tearing slipstream. He began firing at point-blank range at the plunging car alongside, its bumper now locked into the mudguard of the Mercedes. Fairfax, certain now that the other could not escape him, shifted the big car inexorably over to the left-hand verge. He was so intent on forcing the other off the road that he never saw the old Dauphine, yellow headlamps wavering, that was coming peaceably down the wet road towards him. Hypnotized by the blaze of angry headlights streaking at him, the driver stopped in the gutter on his side. Fairfax glancing ahead, saw him no more than fifty yards away. Wrenching the wheel over to the left, he mounted the verge, pushing the Porsche at the same instant off the edge of the road at a point where it was high on a sort of causeway above some bare and rocky ground.

Fairfax was too occupied grappling with the bucking Mercedes as it took to the grass and grazed against the doors on the Dauphine's wrong side. But his passengers caught a glimpse of the Porsche airborne, then languidly turning over before bouncing upside down across the rocks for nearly a hundred yards. The moment it stopped, fierce petrol-fed flames roared up from it.

At last the battered Mercedes stopped skidding, half athwart the road. Fairfax backed it quickly on to the verge, and he and Hans got out.

'I saw Stefan in there, shooting at us,' said Myra. 'I'm coming with you.'

The bent door on her side creaked open. They walked back silently under the cold rain, to stand watching the blaze in the field below from the road edge. The driver of the Dauphine, a middle-aged man, who might have been a commercial traveller going to work early, got out of his car and, pointing an old pistol from his car glove pocket at them, said with cold resolution, 'You are gangsters and murderers. Only by a miracle I am not dead as well. I order you to drive your car directly to the gendarmerie in Gletsch. I shall follow you, and if you attempt to outdistance me, I shall shoot.'

He got into his little car, and brandishing his pistol out of the window, turned it rapidly in the road.

'Well, I suppose we have to sort things out with the authorities sooner or later,' said Fairfax resignedly, turning to walk back to what was left of his car as the Dauphine ground along in the gutter behind them. 'I'm afraid that there's not much we can do for Stefanopoulos or Ulicke now. They were both very brave men, I have to admit.'

'I loved Stefan,' said Myra quietly. 'I believe that most women only have one completely wholehearted and absorbing love in their lives, and he was mine. Sometimes a brute, but always a superman. It's an irresistible combination for a girl.'

Hans put a firm arm round her as she stumbled, brushing tears and rain from her eyes.

Chapter 23

They drove in silence for some way, Fairfax keeping his speed down to about twenty miles an hour so as not to leave the game little Dauphine that was struggling up the hill in their wake. It was rather absurd to think of allowing themselves to be arrested when they not only had a car that could leave the other one standing, but also several machine guns against his old target pistol.

At last Fairfax spoke. 'It's not so much the charges of car-stealing, dangerous driving, assault and so on that bother me,' he said. 'I'm just thinking back to the original charge of murdering you, Peter. Do you think that the fact that you're sitting there, bloody but unbowed, will get me off?'

'I didn't even know about that,' answered Peter, 'but I think I can fix it. I didn't tell you before for obvious reasons, but I'm not mixed up in all this by accident. The British Government had been concerned for some time at the stories of extreme right wing doctors and others assembling at Allerheiligen, so they arranged for me to get work there. I've done a few jobs for them in the past around the world as a respite from hospital medicine. But once there I was never really able to tell them what was going on, even when I finally found out. I was shadowed everywhere, mail was censored, telephones were tapped and my GSM mobile was confiscated, the whole works. That's why I was forced to pinch a car and make a break for it with a spec-imen of their favourite hormone.'

'So you think you can save me from garrotting, or whatever the Swiss do to their murderers?'

'Well,' said Peter, 'judging from the first glimmers of dawn that I can see over there, it must be about four o'clock in the morning. Assuming that we can get the First Secretary of the British Embassy in Berne at such an unearthly hour, it should be possible to get us all out of jail and into a hotel within half an hour.'

'In the midst of all this I'd forgotten a much more pressing prob-lem – right at this moment I'm turning inexorably into a eunuch,' said Fairfax.

'What do you mean?' asked Weldon. 'Did they get some of that hormone into you, then?'

'Yes, they stuck it into my backside right in the middle of one of my best scars.'

'How deep was the wound that made the scar?'

'Right down to the bone. I did it in a motor-cycle crash that went wrong.'

'Then I shouldn't worry about it. The scar tissue is likely to be very poorly vascular, which means that it will have very little circulation through it, and consequently very little absorption from it. If you like we can have a go at it surgically one of these days. It's an oily injec-tion and quite easy to locate.'

'Well, that's the best news I've had for a year or two. Did you hear it, Sally?' Fairfax half-turned his head to smile at her.

'Yes,' she answered. 'You wouldn't expect an ex-continuity girl to miss a vital detail like that, would you?'

'Ex-continuity girl is it, now?' said Fairfax mockingly. 'And to think that this ex-stunt driver was relying on her as his sole future means of support.'